R. J. Par... ...t ...er, editor an... ...to a series of cinematic, high-concept thrillers that ... s the reade... ...om th... ...page and doesn't r... them until the la... R. J. ... ...w lives in Salisb...

richard-parker.com

twitter.com/Bookwalter
facebook.com/RJParkerUK
instagram.com/bemykiller

Also by R. J. Parker

The Dinner Party

While You Slept

THE GOOD NEIGHBOUR

R. J. PARKER

One More Chapter
a division of HarperCollins*Publishers*
1 London Bridge Street
London SE1 9GF
www.harpercollins.co.uk

HarperCollins*Publishers*
1st Floor, Watermarque Building, Ringsend Road
Dublin 4, Ireland

This paperback edition 2021
First published in Great Britain in ebook format
by HarperCollins*Publishers* 2021

A catalogue record of this book is available from the British Library

ISBN: 978-0-00-844796-0

Printed and bound in Great Britain by
CPI Group (UK) Ltd, Croydon CR0 4YY

To Norma and Kayleigh Farrelly – the best neighbours anyone could wish for.

Chapter One

Leah knew exactly where the speed camera was. Even though it was dark, she'd driven home down the country road so many times she was familiar with its gradual curve but never got complacent. She could trust herself but not other drivers. There were no streetlights along Plough Lane but she knew at which overhanging branch to start her slow-down.

There it was – the length of fir illuminated and dipping to the road just after the gated entrance to the old pig farm. She eased the pressure on the accelerator of her mint Fiat 500 and focused on the bend ahead. Traffic came bombing around there, even at this time of night, so she watched for headlights on the curved wall.

Nothing. Looked like it was just her on the road. She passed the beamed cottage where there was one light on upstairs. She'd soon be home and tucked up in bed. Leah wondered if Elliot would be there yet. She glanced at the clock on the dash. At 11.45 she doubted it. He always tried to stay out later than her now. Like it was a competition. As if he was daring Leah to ask him where he'd been.

She knew she'd passed the camera on her left now but didn't pick up speed. Gave it a little longer to make sure. She eventually put her foot on the pedal for a few moments to get her to the bend then took it off as she reached it.

She wouldn't wait up for him, even though she wouldn't sleep until she heard his key in the lock. If he looked in on her she'd close her eyes. Pretend she was asleep. But he probably wouldn't open her door and would go right along the landing to his room as noisily as possible. Leah tried to recall how long ago it had been since she'd waited for him to get undressed before she entered his room. They'd had sex, that's all it had been, fulfilling a need before she'd counted the minutes and left him in his single bed. He hadn't asked her to stay.

She had turned thirty in the summer and didn't know how much longer she was going to allow herself to hang on for something that might already be over. Elliot wasn't in denial of that but Leah felt an almost physical blow to her stomach when she imagined saying goodbye to him. And it wasn't just because she was afraid of leaving the security of the life and home they'd created together. After eight years, she still loved him but how much longer could she when he'd become so distant?

Leah went rigid as the curved wall in front of her was suddenly lit up. A motorcyclist shot around the bend quickly after and her fingers tightened on the steering wheel. The bike was in the middle of the road, its rider probably assuming it would be deserted.

She decelerated, tried to anticipate his reaction. He was still coming straight at her. Leah steered sharply left and hoped the motorcyclist didn't do the same.

He cut to her right, but Leah had almost reached him. She was going to catch his back wheel. Leah's headlights revealed his battered red biker's jacket and glinted off the visor of his black helmet.

She clenched herself in readiness for the impact and heard an incoherent exclamation from herself and an aggressive one from him as he swung his bike away from her and buzzed close by her window.

Leah waited for the scrape of metal but miraculously he passed her without contact. She kept her attention locked on the road ahead. She was about to hit the bend and tugged the wheel hard so she wouldn't collide with the wall.

If the car had been travelling any faster she would have hit it but she slowed right down as she reached it and came to a standstill a few feet from the bricks and wondered if there were any other vehicles coming the other way. No sign of any.

Leah glanced in her mirror. The bike had righted itself and was speeding in the opposite direction. The motorcyclist wasn't hanging about to find out if she was OK. If he carried on riding like that, he'd be a statistic before long.

Leah's heart felt like it was bouncing around her chest. It was just her on the bend, engine puttering. She checked her mirror again and watched the red light of the bike vanish into darkness. It was a still night, light drizzle suspended in the headlights as if it were holding its breath. Leah could hear the buzz of the motor but was sure he wasn't coming back.

She breathed out, dropped her shoulders a little, accelerated forward and picked up speed as she got on the straight road that took her to the traffic lights. Leah briefly closed her eyes.

She was barely doing forty but when she opened them again there was no time to avoid the shape that darted in front of her. Two eyes glinted silver as the car harshly struck flesh and bone.

Chapter Two

Leah gasped as her seat belt cut into her and, momentarily, the impact made her lose hold of the wheel. It felt like the car was spinning and as she clamped both hands back onto the rubber grip, she could see only darkness ahead. Was she about to crash into the wall? Her foot was jammed on the brake, but she was still moving.

A row of bushes swung into view and Leah's body jerked sideways as the Fiat abruptly halted. She cried out as her neck snapped still.

After a few seconds she opened her eyes and her first thought was other traffic. She quickly took in her position on the road. She was half off it, the front part of her vehicle in the briers. She turned and saw the bulk of the animal she'd collided with on the right-hand side. It was a deer. She'd seen it for a split second before the car had struck it, eyes lit up by the headlights and antlers illuminated before she'd hit it full on. Leah could see them now, partially sticking up from the road like a gnarled tree growing out of its body.

Her head swivelled back the other way and the pain of doing so made her suck in air. No oncoming vehicles but that might not be the case for long. The engine was still running although the sound seemed muted. Leah tried to accelerate forward so the back of her car wasn't in the road. She rolled about a foot, but a dry rubbing sound emerged from the front of the Fiat before it stopped.

Even when she put the pedal almost to the floor, Leah couldn't accelerate or reverse. She quickly undid her seat belt and as its pressure was released, she experienced a shooting pain in her abdomen. She breathed in and out a few times and it didn't seem to get any worse. She had to move the car. If someone came tearing down the road, they might not see the rear of hers in time.

She opened the door and got out, staggering sideways on the uneven marshy grass at the side of the road. The mud squelched as her boots sank. It was freezing cold and the smell of soil was in her nostrils. Her soles squeaked on the wet blades as she negotiated the open driver's door and moved around the front of the mint-green car to examine the damage.

She slid in the muck and supported herself on the front of the car, but the metallic surface was slick, and she knew what the warmth on her fingers was. Her headlights lit up the dark red covering the palm of her hand, but she fought repulsion and the instinct to wipe it on the grass. The car had to be shifted quickly but as she leaned down to examine the left wheel, she could see the arch was crushed against the tyre.

Leah tried to prise the green metal away from the rubber. It wouldn't give and she grunted with the exertion as the edge of the arch cut into her fingers and almost drew some of her own blood.

She went quickly to the rear of the car and opened the door. The kit for changing the tyre was there and she took out the wheel wrench and trod gingerly back to the front. After three attempts she managed to lever the crushed arch off the wheel, but she still wasn't sure if it was enough to allow it to turn.

Leah dropped into the driver's seat and put her foot on the accelerator. The car went forward half a foot but stopped again. Was the tyre still jammed or was it just slipping in the mud? The back of the car was still on the road. 'Come on!' She put the pedal right to the floor. 'Move!'

The Fiat suddenly shot forward and before she could lift her foot the front of the vehicle tipped forward. Leah slammed against the steering wheel as the car struck something solid.

She'd slid the Fiat down a shallow bank and now the front of the car was resting in the shallow stream of a ditch. She switched off the engine and suddenly it was pitch black. Nothing but the low mutter of the water. As her eyes became accustomed to the weak moonlight, she reached for her handbag that she'd left on the passenger seat. No sign. She scrabbled her hand about in the footwell and was relieved to find it there. Quickly clambering out of the car she shut the door and stumbled back.

The car was definitely off the road now but as she took out her phone, she confirmed what she already knew. The battery was flat. The screen didn't even light up. She'd tried to charge it on the train, but the plug point had had chewing gum stuffed in it. She slid it back into her bag and ascended the slope to the roadside.

As she emerged from the bushes the thorny branches clung to her black woollen sweater. She extricated herself and looked up and down the road. Still no other cars in either direction. Her attention shifted to the dark shape about thirty feet away from her on the other side of the road. Her breath caught. In the darkness she could make out a small silver cloud rising from it. The deer was still alive.

Walking through the mist of her uneven panting, Leah crossed over and tentatively followed the wall to where the animal lay. This was dangerous. There was no walkway, just the edge of the road and no time to cross if a car shot around the bend. But she couldn't leave the deer if it was still alive. It would get hit again. And the next car might have an even more serious accident.

She picked up her pace. Shivered against the cold. She'd left her jacket in the car but didn't consider going back to get it. Her stomach trembled and ached, but her attention was fixed on the prostrate shape and the sporadic vapour emerging from it into the night air.

She was about twelve feet away from it when it stopped. She did as well. Waited. And hated herself for hoping that no more emerged.

Leah held her breath.

No more came.

She released hers. But she had to move the animal. Couldn't leave it there. As she got closer, she could see that the antler sticking up had been snapped and one half of it was hanging down. She squinted into the gloom. It was pointless trying to use the torch on her phone.

As she reached the deer, she listened for any sound of it breathing but there was nothing. She could smell it now though. A musty aroma with a sour and pungent edge. Through the gloom she could see its head was at an unnatural angle to its body. And another section of its antlers lay in the road behind it.

The bulk of its body and its rear quarters were against the wall. If she could just move the head off the road, she could be sure it wouldn't cause any cars to swerve. And she could alert the police of its presence there as soon as she got hold of a phone.

She trotted by the animal and picked up the piece of antler that was lying there. She held it for a few moments. It felt heavy and smooth. Leah threw it over the wall and felt a pang of guilt. But she had to make sure it wasn't a hazard to other motorists.

She returned to the front of the animal, exhaled and then bent down and put her hand on the thick fur of its forehead. It was still warm, and she held it for a moment, waiting to feel any reaction to her touch. The deer didn't twitch. Leah tensed her stomach and slid the head so it was in line with the rest of the body against the wall. She used the broken antlers to quickly push it into position there.

Leah stood, blood pounding in her ears. She had to

inhale and when she did, took in its aroma again. She felt sick but fought the nausea and turned back towards the car. She wasn't about to get it out of the ditch, so it looked like she'd have to walk all the way along Plough Lane until she reached the traffic lights at the edge of her village. A cold wind gusted towards Leah as if warning her against taking the route.

But as the current agitated the trees, she caught the twinkle of a light up ahead and to the right. She knew what it was. There was a house there. She'd never glimpsed the building because it was hidden behind high wooden gates at the front but there was a spherical light outside that lit them up at night.

Leah started to walk swiftly in its direction and wondered if there was anybody home.

Chapter Three

L eah strode towards the light. She was still very exposed on the road and wanted to get off it as soon as possible. The aroma of the deer was still potent in her nostrils, and her neck and abdomen ached. She knew she was probably in shock but, until she spoke to Elliot, nobody knew where she was.

Just over a minute later she could see the yellow spherical light on a metal pole. Its glass had a faint green tinge from the overhanging trees, but it sufficiently illuminated the tall wooden gates behind it. Maybe they'd be shut tight. They looked to be the sort that had electric locks.

But as she approached, she could see that one of them was slightly pushed inward. Leah put her hand on the cold metal loop set in the gate and shoved. To her relief it swung in easily and she was standing in a gravelled courtyard in front of a very modern three-storey house. Much of its frontage was glass and the small percentage of wall visible appeared to be made of a dark slate. Bare wisteria branches twisted along the guttering beneath the roof and three green plastic overflow barrels were positioned below. A dark blue car and a silver car were parked to the left of the property.

There were lights on in the downstairs and upstairs rooms and the gravel was sufficiently lit for her as she noisily crossed it to the wide canary-yellow front door. She examined the frame for a doorbell, couldn't see one, so urgently rapped the heavy knocker three times.

No sound from within. Maybe whoever lived here was in bed and left the lights on as a deterrent. Leah knocked again. She waited, strained her ears and realised how fast her circulation was still pumping.

Rain started falling harder and she turned back to the gate as a car sped past. She waited for the sound of their engine to recede. The body of the deer clearly hadn't been an obstruction. The canopy of trees over the courtyard twitched as fat droplets burst on the gravel.

The door clicked and Leah turned, relief filtering through her as it started to open. She just needed a phone. It halted briefly, as if the owner were hesitating, then it swung wide.

A man was standing in the doorway and briefly Leah didn't know how to begin. His features frowned at her, fair brows knitted over pure green eyes. But his expression wasn't hostile. He was probably in his early forties but maybe it was his deep tan that made him appear older. Fine yellow hair covered his ears, almost touching his shoulders, and was parted to neatly frame his face.

'I'm so sorry to knock on your door at this time of night.'

He didn't respond but patiently raised his eyebrows.

'The gate was ajar and you're the nearest house.'

'Are you … OK?' His face wrinkled in concern.

Leah realised she was clenching her fists, which she always did when she was trying to keep it together. She did it a lot when she was talking to Elliot. 'Just a little shaken. My car hit a deer just back there on the road.'

His mouth formed an 'oh' shape.

Leah didn't give him time to speak. 'It's dead but I managed to pull it out of the way. I need to let the police know because it might be a hazard to other drivers. My car's off the road too. The wheel's damaged. I tried to free it, but it rolled down into the ditch.' *Too much info. Stick to why you're here, Leah.* 'My phone battery is flat. Could I please borrow your phone or just plug mine in?'

He was already stepping back to let her enter.

'I couldn't charge it on the train. I tried to. I just need to let my husband know where I am.'

He was nodding, gesturing her into the brightly lit hallway. 'Of course, come out of the rain. Do you need me to call you an ambulance?'

'No, I think I'm fine, thanks.' Leah stepped inside the house. An exotic savoury dinner aroma hit her at the same time as the warm atmosphere. 'So sorry to disturb you.'

He shook his head. 'Phone's right there.' He closed the door and indicated the small table beside it where a handset stood in a charging unit.

'I've got the plug for this.' She took the phone out of her handbag.

He waved that away. 'Use it to make whatever call you need.' But his eyes dropped to her hand.

In the hallway light she could now see how much thick blood daubed the heel of it and the sleeve of her jumper. 'Oh God. It was all over the car.'

His green eyes darted between her hand and the phone unit. 'Maybe clean yourself first. In there.' He nodded to a door beside the coats hanging on the wall.

'If you wouldn't mind, thank you. I'll be very quick.' She put her phone back in her handbag.

'It's no problem. Take your time.'

'One minute.' A light came on automatically when she opened the door. The room behind it was bigger than Leah expected but still only contained a toilet and a sink. She entered, closed it behind her and put her handbag on the shelf under the mirror. She turned on the tap and water ran down the length of half a shiny open steel pipe and trickled into the dark slate sink. She'd left blood on the chrome tap but concentrated on cleaning her hand first. The water turned red as it flowed from her fingers. Leah held the edge of her sleeve under the stream and squeezed the black wool. It was saturated and the water went darker.

She took a breath and felt her stomach smart. Catching her reflection in the mirror in front of her Leah was shocked at her transformation. Her pinched, white and grubby complexion looked deathly pale. Her dark brown locks had been neatly straightened and clipped to the top of her head when she'd got in the car at the station but now hung at the sides of her head. She removed the gold clip and released her hair, but it had already curled and clumped in the damp air. She looked deranged. And despite the welcoming smell of the house the aroma of the deer was still about her face.

Leah turned on the warm tap and the heat travelled through her from her fingers. She splashed some onto her face. Rubbed it around the edges of her nostrils. Her fingers shook while she did it.

'OK in there?'

She rubbed her aching neck. 'Fine. Coming now.' After cleaning the tap, Leah took the tan towel hanging on the brass warmer rack beside the sink and dried her face. It smelt of coconut and, momentarily, she wanted to leave it there. She quickly dried her hands. They were clean now, but the sleeve felt cold and heavy on her arm. She pulled it down and wrung it out, dried her arm then replaced the towel as neatly as she could.

Leah took a breath, picked up her handbag and then walked back into the hallway.

The owner was just relaying his address. He hung up. 'I hope you don't mind. I just called the police.'

Chapter Four

'Oh ... thank you.' Was that because of the blood on her hand or was he just being helpful?

'Told them you've pranged a deer. They're sending a patrol car as soon as they can but said it might be a while.'

'I'm worried somebody else might hit it. As I said, I did drag it away from the road. Can I quickly call my husband?'

'Of course.' He extended his tanned hand and the phone.

Leah took it from him. 'Thanks.' She quickly dialled Elliot's mobile and pursed her lips while she waited for a reply, taking in her host a little more. He was wearing a smart navy-blue shirt, open at the collar, black slacks held up by a belt with a gold buckle, and a pair of casual bottle-green linen slip-ons with white rubber soles that looked incongruous with the rest of the outfit. Clearly his comfy home footwear.

Elliot's phone went to his answering service. She waited for the robotic voice to finish telling her that the person she

17

was calling was unavailable and waited for the beep. 'Elliot. It's just me.' Her tone was neutral. She smiled at her host who remained in the hallway. Behind him was a staircase carpeted in sage green. 'I've had a little accident in the car. Nothing serious but I might be home later. I'll explain everything to you then.' She hung up. 'Thank you.' She handed the phone to him. 'Sorry, I didn't even introduce myself. I'm Leah Talbot.'

'Martin Tate.'

There was an awkward moment as they both considered if they should make the introduction official.

'I understand if you don't want to shake hands. I live just up the road, in Forley. Have been for the past seven years. In Minster Street. Near the railway bridge.' *Too much information again, Leah.*

He regarded her blankly.

'By the Black Horse Inn.'

Recognition flickered in his eyes. 'Yes. I do know it.'

'I sometimes drive past here on my way to the station and I've always wondered what's behind these gates.' *Oh God, that sounded stalky.*

He smiled kindly. 'So, we're virtually neighbours.'

'Yes. Pretty close neighbours.' Leah told herself to dial it back. She'd be producing her passport in a moment.

'Are you sure you're OK?' He squinted at her suspiciously.

'Fine.' She took a breath. 'Just ... shaken, I think.'

'Can I at least help you get your car back on the road?'

She took in his groomed appearance. 'No. I wouldn't

want to drag you out into the rain. Besides, I don't think it'll move very far.'

'By calling roadside repair, I meant.' A smile briefly registered as he brandished the phone. 'I don't have a lot of experience in car mechanics.'

'Of course. I'm with the AA but I think I left my card in the car.' She rummaged through her handbag but knew it wouldn't be there. Now her legs felt wobbly.

'No problem. I could use mine and they can sort you out when they arrive. I don't think you should be going back out there. This road's treacherous enough in the daytime.'

'That would be very kind.'

'So your husband, he's not at home?'

'No, he's out tonight.'

'On Valentine's night?' Martin Tate seemed surprised.

Valentine's Day. She'd forgotten about that. It hadn't had any significance for the past couple of years. She was about to make a scoffing comment but stopped herself. 'Yes,' she answered simply. He didn't need any hints about her home life.

'Come and have a seat. I hope you don't mind me saying but you're looking a bit pale.'

'That's OK.' She held up a hand. 'I've disturbed your evening enough.' Her gaze went to the lit kitchen beyond.

'It's no problem. Just me here.' He'd read her mind.

'You live here alone?'

'Put it this way, you're not disturbing a romantic dinner.'

That wasn't an answer. Leah heard a small internal alarm bell. Her car was down the road and she hadn't told

Elliot in her message that she was inside a stranger's house on Plough Lane.

'Come and sit down while I call the AA.'

Despite feeling light-headed, Leah nodded but didn't move.

He obviously sensed her unease. 'Does my cooking smell that bad?'

Leah was about to smile but at that moment a dog came down the stairs. It was a white and brown basset hound and its ears flapped about its head as it descended awkwardly.

'He doesn't bite either.'

The animal slid down the last few green stairs on its stomach and made a beeline for Leah.

She bent to pet the dog. 'What's his name?'

'Her. It's Sheila.'

She tried to pat its head while it snuffled at her jeans. 'Hi, Sheila.' Leah held out her hand so Sheila could sniff it, but the dog ignored her. She stood up but felt giddy and staggered back.

'Whoa.' Tate caught her firmly by the arm.

He had a very tight grip but as soon as she'd regained her balance, he released her.

'Sorry.' He pulled both his arms in as if he shouldn't have touched her.

'That's OK. I think I do need to sit down though, if you wouldn't mind.'

'Just in here.' He immediately turned and led her towards the doorway of the kitchen.

Leah followed and found herself in a very impressive and modern space. More dark slate walls were broken up by bright white splash tiles behind the huge sink and cooking range. In the middle was a long breakfast bar and several stools. A half-eaten meal lay on it with a full bowl-glass of red wine beside it.

Leah's scalp prickled cold. 'I'm sorry. I've interrupted your dinner.' Her mouth felt dry.

'Not at all.' He pulled out a stool. 'Sit yourself down.'

But Leah stumbled, fell and blacked out before she reached it.

Chapter Five

Leah drew breath in anticipation of the fall and then realised she was sitting on an armchair in a completely different room. She sat bolt upright and grunted as her neck and stomach reminded her of the crash. Martin Tate held out a placatory palm to her. He was seated in an armchair opposite. He had the phone in his other hand.

'Sure you wouldn't like me to call you an ambulance?'

'What time is it?' Leah took in the lounge she was in. A large blank TV screen was mounted on the powder-blue wall before her and there was an ornate dresser covered with framed family photos to her left. To her right was an occasional table. Tate had placed her handbag there.

'It's OK. You've barely been out a minute.'

Leah swallowed and rubbed her face.

'I just caught you in time. You completely folded.'

'I'm sorry.'

'Don't apologise. You're obviously still in shock.'

'I've taken up enough of your time.' Leah tried to stand but immediately felt dizzy again.

'Just stay there,' he said firmly then smiled. 'Take a breath. I really don't have anything more important to do this evening. Are you sure you don't want someone to take a look at you?'

She shook her head. 'I've got low blood pressure. It happens sometimes. Especially if I get out of bed too quickly.' But Leah suspected there had been more to her blackout than that. The trauma of another car accident was never far from her thoughts.

He nodded then rose.

Leah felt a little uncomfortable as he looked thoughtfully down at her.

'I'll call the breakdown people, just stay there.' Tate walked out of the room, the phone at his ear.

Leah listened to him opening some cupboards in the kitchen while he relayed the situation to the AA and gave them his card number and address details. She felt so foolish but as she gripped the arms of the chair her vision fizzed yellow. Despite the obvious presence of an air freshener she could still smell the deer. She tipped her head forward to get some blood back into it.

'Here.'

She looked up and found Tate standing in front of her. She hadn't heard him re-enter the room.

'Do you like brandy? I don't really know if it steadies nerves but that's the extent of my first-aid skills, I'm afraid.' He offered a cut-glass tumbler of it to her.

'Not really.'

'How about a glass of red. I've got a bottle open.'

'I don't drink red wine. Too acidic for me. This'll be fine, thanks.' She took it from him.

'Truck's going to take five to ten minutes.' He seated himself again, leaning back in the armchair and crossing his leg. 'They're coming here first. Or I could drop you home now if you're not feeling up to it.'

'I'll be fine in a moment, really.' She broke the silence by taking a gulp of the brandy. She swallowed too much of it and it burnt the back of her throat. Leah just managed to stifle a choke.

Amusement played about his features again. 'Can I get you some water or a hot drink?'

'No, this is good.' And it actually was. Leah normally hated brown spirits, like the whisky that Elliot collected and revered, but she could feel the liquid warming her all the way down and took another careful sip.

'Do you want to try your husband again?'

She shook her head definitively.

Tate frowned.

'He won't be back yet.' She couldn't keep the dismissive tone from her voice.

'He will be though?'

Leah nodded.

'I don't like to think of you going home to an empty house after you've had such an ordeal.'

'I'll be fine. Honestly. Maybe I should go and wait outside.'

Tate gritted his teeth. 'I'm sorry. I didn't mean to make you uncomfortable.'

'You didn't.' She slid to the edge of the seat. 'You've been very kind.'

'Your choice. At least charge your phone before you go.' He nodded to her handbag.

She was shakily standing. 'That's OK. Now the breakdown guy is on the way I can charge it when I get home.'

'It's still raining hard out there.'

It made sense to stay where she was, charge the phone and wait for the police and the breakdown truck in the house. Why was she so determined to leave? She lifted her handbag up by the strap and slung it over her shoulder. 'Thank you for this.' She placed the empty tumbler of brandy carefully on the glass-topped table.

Tate stood but didn't respond.

'I'll be fine. I shouldn't have knocked on your door—' Leah felt her legs crumple the way they had in the kitchen.

He darted forward and caught her by her elbows, his grip firm as before.

Leah attempted to straighten but it was him supporting her.

'Take a breath.'

She looked up at him, saw something beyond his concerned expression.

'You'll be fine.'

Her eyes were on his mouth and she felt an almost irresistible compulsion.

Chapter Six

Their lips gently touched and Leah remained in his grip for a few seconds. Wanted to stay there. His mouth was warm. When had Elliot last embraced her? But then she tensed up and he released her.

'I'm sorry.' Tate took a pace back.

Leah looked down at his slip-ons.

'That was inexcusable.'

She shook her head, still didn't make eye contact with him. Had he kissed her? Her mouth had met his.

'That's not … it's not how I usually behave...'

Her shoulders remained bunched, her gaze still at his feet. But shouldn't she be apologising too? She looked up at him.

'The police are already on their way if you'd like to report me for harassment.'

Leah hefted her handbag again. 'I'll wait by the gates, if that's OK.'

He nodded, seemed to know she'd made up her mind. 'OK. Let me at least give you an umbrella though.'

Leah nodded once, relieved he was making her exit from the house easy. He gestured her ahead and followed her back into the hallway.

'One of these?' Leah asked politely, as if she couldn't still taste his mouth on hers, and pointed to an assortment of umbrellas in a stand below the coat rack. Her ears felt boiling hot.

'Whichever one you want,' he replied stiltedly.

Leah picked up the nearest. It was a red ladies' umbrella.

'Take a larger one.' Tate extracted a longer beige one and handed it to her.

She took it. 'I'll leave it on the doorstep when I'm finished, if that's OK.' She was looking at his chest.

'You really can wait here in the dry.'

She switched her focus to the door. 'I've disturbed your Friday enough.'

'I'll just finish my dinner and you can sit here.' He indicated the ornate gold cushioned armchair to the immediate right of the door.

'Some fresh air will probably be good for me.' She had to leave now but stopped in front of the door. There were a couple of locks on it. Could she just get out by turning the knob?

'OK.' Tate leaned around her, being careful not to invade her space. He opened the door and revealed the wall of water on the other side. It was torrential.

Leah moved to the doorstep and opened the umbrella. Droplets pelted noisily against it.

'I really hope it's not my fault you're running away.'

'I'd really prefer to be here to meet the breakdown truck.' She stepped onto the gravel and stood back, so they weren't at close quarters. Leah met his green eyes.

He nodded, resignedly.

'I'll leave the umbrella on the doorstep,' Leah repeated.

'Don't worry about that. Stay dry. Drop it back to me when you're done.'

'I'll be fine,' she said flatly. But part of her didn't want their conversation to be over.

'Don't worry. I'll tell the police exactly what's happened. Minster Street?'

'Number thirty-three.' Should she really be telling him that?

'Thirty-three. Got it. Nice to meet you, Leah Talbot.'

That seemed odd to Leah. Using her surname, as if he were proving he'd remembered.

He smiled lopsidedly. 'Give me a shout if you need help.'

She turned and strode away.

He closed the door and suddenly the courtyard seemed very dark. Leah turned and walked past the two parked cars to the gates. Had his offer re returning the umbrella been what she thought it was? Did her want her to come back with it? She dismissed the thought.

The wet wind blew hard against her and she could feel the cold rain soaking the tops of her jeans. But at that moment she heard an engine slow and yellow lights shone through the gap in the gates. Leah quickened her pace, pushed through and found a breakdown vehicle pulling up outside.

The balding, middle-aged driver rolled down his window and squinted against the rain. 'Breakdown?'

'Yes. Man who lived here called you. My card is in the car.'

'And where's that?'

'About a hundred yards down there.'

'All right, sweetheart, just hop in and we'll take a look.'

'Just two seconds.' Leah held up her hand. She ducked back through the gates and crossed the courtyard again. Thankfully, she couldn't see any sign of Tate at any of the windows. Leah quickly folded down the beige umbrella, left it against the door and then dashed back to the breakdown truck.

Chapter Seven

When Leah got home the house was in darkness. Even though he might have switched off the lights before turning in, she resisted the temptation to call Elliot's name. Was that because she felt guilty about what had just happened? Could she really face him now? She hadn't kissed anybody else in eight years. As she'd been driven home, she hadn't heard a word the driver had said, had tried to dissect just why she'd succumbed to the moment. It was so unlike anything she'd ever done. The trauma of the accident aside, was it Martin Tate's kindness towards her that had precipitated it? If she'd been male would he have showed the same generosity towards a stranger? She walked to the door on the left side of the kitchen, opened it and switched on the bulb there.

No blue Vauxhall in the garage. Elliot was still out.

This was no surprise to her, but it was a disappointment she didn't want tonight. She really wanted his presence but some Fridays he didn't come home at all. The first time, he'd dismissively told her he'd stayed with a friend in London. After that, she hadn't asked. He did it because he wanted her to, so she didn't. But the truth was she worried about him. Maybe he *was* just staying with friends. There didn't seem to be any indication he was seeing somebody else. Perhaps he was just good at concealing it from her though. He commuted to an environmental consultancy in Canada Square and Leah no longer had any idea with whom he worked or socialised.

She walked into the cold lounge and switched on the light there too. The bulb emitted a low buzz that accentuated how silent the house was except for the patter of the rain on the windows. Her laptop was still open on the table in front of the black double-glazed panes. Everything as it was since she'd left it there that morning. She picked up her empty coffee cup and plate and carried them to the kitchen.

As she checked the back door was secured, she experienced a familiar sensation and knew it was why she'd acted so out of character that night. Leah often felt completely alone. And it would continue that way even when Elliot got back. Having him in the house but isolated from her made Leah feel even more secluded. She tried to brush the toast crumbs from her plate into the bin, but they'd dried on the china and her fingernails scratched the rough surface before she gave up and put it in the sink. That was one thing they still had conversations about. Elliot regularly complained that he was tired of tidying away her dishes. He still made two meals a day, but she was a grazer, sporadically grabbing something while she pored over accounts for the two property management companies she worked remotely for.

Today had been one of the occasions she'd had to go to the office. Nothing had been discussed that they couldn't have put in an email but once every two months, they liked to drag her up to HQ to remind themselves what she looked like. She preferred being closeted at home and what had just happened proved why. Again, the smell of the deer wafted over her. She checked her hands and clothes. *Get that jumper off.*

Leah went upstairs to the bathroom, stripped off and put all her clothes in the washing bin. She got into the shower and turned it on. It was freezing. The hot water hadn't been on all day. The shower head squealed. It was blocked, needed descaling. She reminded herself to do it every time she stood there.

It was the sort of chore Elliot would have done in a flash before. There were a lot of jobs that weren't getting done now though and the disrepair of the house reflected their emotional situation. She waited, shivering outside the jets until it eventually came through warm. She let them play weakly over her face and thoroughly washed her nose out again. She wiped at her lips and thought of the moment Martin Tate had leaned down to her. She kept on shivering but she wasn't cold. He'd been right. She was probably still in shock. That poor animal she'd hit. Leah thought about its last breath escaping in a cloud. Would the police remove it tonight?

Leah slid down the wall and stayed sitting in the shower longer than she should have, lingering in the heat and steam and thinking about another incident on a road many years earlier, her fingers on a warm face. Bruises of grief and anger that were always there began to ache again. She put her arms around herself and thought of the brief embrace she'd had less than an hour earlier.

Just as she'd finished drying herself and her hair, she heard a door slam. She quickly slipped on her peach towelling robe. It seemed ludicrous being modest in her marital home but that was where they were at. Neither of them walked around naked in front of each other anymore. She cracked the door and felt the cold air sucked in from the landing. 'Elliot?'

No response.

Leah tied the belt about her robe and stepped onto the landing. 'Elliot?' she said louder.

The rain on the skylight was deafening.

A thud from downstairs.

'Elliot!' He had to have heard her. But, as he'd pointed out recently, he didn't have to answer to her anymore.

She walked barefoot to the top of the stairs and looked down them. Light was spilling along the hallway from the open lounge door. She opened her mouth to call his name again but thought better of it. She descended the stairs and walked into the kitchen. Nobody there.

A creak from the lounge.

Leah made her way into the room and found Elliot lying on the couch. He didn't have his glasses on and was squinting at the TV remote.

'Didn't you hear me?'

He nodded and returned his attention to the buttons.

His mop of fair hair looked dishevelled and he was still wearing his blue work suit that looked as crumpled as he did. She could smell the beer. 'You drove home.'

'No.' It seemed to be his only response but then he added: 'Scooter man drove me.'

She eyed the glass of red wine and greasy bag of food on the coffee table but didn't say anything.

'Where's *your* car?' he retorted.

'Didn't you get my message?'

He took out his phone.

'It's been towed.' She let that sink in.

He sighed. 'Clamped?'

'No. I had an accident. Driving back along Plough Lane.'

That seemed to penetrate his drunken haze. His expression looked shocked but then the hardness was back in his regard. 'You're obviously all right.'

Leah tried not to react to his indifference. But it hurt her deeply. How had he become this? Elliot was a sensitive man. More empathetic than she was. He'd cared deeply for her, had defended her – too much sometimes. And now he went out of his way to show Leah the barriers he'd built against her. It was an act, but it was such an ugly one.

He seemed to realise he'd been too cold, sat upright and ditched the remote. 'What happened?'

'I hit a deer. Killed it.'

He nodded, soberly. 'Any other cars involved?'

'No. The breakdown truck dropped me off and they took the Fiat off for repairs.'

He looked relieved. 'All taken care of then?'

She nodded. 'I'm going to bed.' Leah turned on her heel.

Elliot started to say something else, but she pulled the door after her and walked back upstairs.

He didn't follow.

Half an hour later she was still lying awake in bed with her bedside lamp on, the events of the evening playing over in her head. The last breath of the deer and Martin Tate's mouth covering hers.

A light knock on the door.

Leah pulled her duvet up. 'Yes?'

Elliot poked his head around the door and, for one moment, looked like the man she'd known before their problems had started. His expression was cowed, apologetic. 'Permission to enter?'

She didn't respond but waited for him to walk in.

He did but remained in the doorway. 'Are you OK, really?'

She nodded. 'Fine. Just shaken.' Her neck and abdomen protested. 'Maybe a bit of whiplash.'

'I should call an ambulance.'

'No, I've already … I decided against that.'

'Let me call you a cab to take you to A & E.'

'Honestly, I really do feel fine. I promise I'll go in the morning if I feel any worse. Right now, I'm just exhausted.'

'OK. Let me know if you change your mind.' He frowned with genuine concern. 'Was there much damage to the car?'

'The wheel arch was crushed.' Should she tell him how

she'd had to push it off the road and it had ended up in the ditch, that a complete stranger had been the only person who had helped her? 'The insurance will cover it.'

He stiffened. 'That's not why I'm asking.'

She knew it wasn't.

'If you're sure you're OK.'

'I've had a shower and I feel much better.' She wanted to tell him she was still trembling. But that would pass. 'Don't worry. Go to bed.'

But Elliot didn't budge from the door. He appeared to be turning something over in his head. 'I know … things are really strange at the moment. *This* is really strange.' He gestured around the room as he struggled to articulate himself.

Leah waited.

Elliot walked over to the bed.

Leah could see the old Elliot in his eyes.

But he stopped short of the embrace that should have followed and touched the back of her hand.

'Hope you can sleep.' He squeezed her fingers.

His felt warm before he released her.

Leah didn't react and watched him turn, walk out of the room and close the door quietly behind him.

Chapter Eight

The next morning Leah woke early, unsettling images and sensations from the night before vying to greet her – the dying animal at the roadside jolting against what she'd allowed to happen in Martin Tate's lounge. Her neck and stomach only vaguely ached now but she remained in bed. Elliot was meant to be getting up early for a run. He was training for an ironman in July. His father had coronary issues but he'd stridently dismissed her worries. She wondered how trying to make your heart explode for seventeen straight hours couldn't lead to health problems in the future. He was obviously drinking while he was training as well.

She knew, after his late Friday, he definitely wouldn't be out at six as he was in the week, but she heard him stagger into the bathroom just before seven. Would he even remember his visit to her room the previous night? He'd been quite drunk, and she wondered if he was chastising himself for allowing her a glimpse of the real Elliot. Seeing his old self soak through made her realise just how much she missed him.

Leah didn't want to bump into him when he was hungover though. She listened to him go downstairs and then clatter about the kitchen. A few minutes later the front door slammed. He wouldn't be back for a good few hours. Maybe they could talk properly tonight. They used to share everything, never withheld from each other. At least, that's what she'd assumed. Would he even care about a confession though or just use it as another excuse to close himself off from her?

She rose and brushed her teeth. She'd only recently showered and was relieved she could no longer smell the deer. The notion of staying in her pyjamas for the morning was tempting. Working from home had made her way too fond of that. She wandered downstairs to the kitchen.

She looked through the window to the overgrown garden. The rain had stopped, and the sky was blue but it looked cold. She got herself a bowl of granola and chewed a few mouthfuls, but the echo of her crunching made her move into the lounge.

She put on News 24 and sat on the couch. Elliot's empty wine glass and greasy unidentifiable meat in bread lay half-eaten on top of its paper bag in the middle of the coffee table. Saturdays used to be their favourite day. Bagels and Americano together, jobs around the house and then usually out with friends in the evening. Both their groups of friends had halved now. They'd all declared a side but neither she nor Elliot got invited out as much. She supposed everyone was uncomfortable with the self-imposed limbo they were in. There had been no affair. No flashpoint. Elliot had just told her he didn't feel the same way about her.

She'd thought that had been his way of breaking away from her so he could see somebody else but still nobody had materialised. Maybe that had been his game plan from the start. To make it go on so long that when he did bring somebody into the picture it would seem like a natural progression and not something that had been premeditated. Did he expect her to just walk out at some point so he could start the life he wanted with whoever was waiting patiently on the sideline? Leah almost hoped that was the truth because the alternative was what he'd told her nearly two years ago: he just didn't love her anymore.

Her friends told her to leave. Elliot was the only one who hadn't. But his behaviour was engineered to achieve the same outcome. There were moments, like last night, when it briefly felt like it had before. In that past she'd taken the permanence of what they'd had for granted. Saturday afternoons only meant looking after her father now, however. His condition had markedly deteriorated in the last year but the one good thing about her situation was that she could devote more hours to him without it having to be an issue with Elliot.

Leah put her bowl on the table. She listened to the weather forecast but didn't hear it. She didn't want to finish chewing her last mouthful because then she'd have to decide what to do next. Work for the morning? She already used her new surfeit of time to get well ahead of schedule. The hours she no longer spent being a wife were considerable and she now delivered her accounts early. No more Sunday nights staying up late after a long weekend away to make sure she just met a deadline. She'd hated that pressure and panic but now she yearned for it. Her life was now a well-ordered and punctual vacuum.

She rubbed her shoulders through her white cotton pyjamas and came to a decision.

Leah went back upstairs and pulled on a pair of jeans and a powder-blue sweatshirt. She felt better just being dressed. Then she straightened her hair. Took more time over it than usual and put on a touch of makeup. She never wore much and couldn't remember the last occasion she had.

Heading back downstairs, she turned off the TV and slipped on a pair of black suede boots. She grabbed Elliot's car keys then paused. She went back into the kitchen and selected a bottle of Malbec from the rack.

This was the best thing to do. Get back behind a wheel. As she pulled out into the road, she was surprised not to feel more nervous. Reaching the end of Minster Street Leah knew exactly which way she was turning.

She headed back to Plough Lane. The house where she'd met Martin Tate was less than five minutes away. That was why she'd made herself presentable. As well as dropping off the bottle of red to thank him (she knew he drank it), what else did she expect? She'd left abruptly after he'd helped her out. It was obvious why so she wouldn't apologise for that but what if he invited her inside again?

The wine on the passenger seat was an excuse. She couldn't fool herself about that. And last night Elliot had showed her tenderness that he hadn't for some time. She took her foot off the accelerator. *What are you thinking? This is stupid. Turn around, go back home.*

A car behind her beeped as it decelerated to avoid hitting her.

'Sorry.' She mouthed in her mirror and held up her hand. She picked up speed again. *OK, the decision has been made.* Leah decided she would drive past the house and check the deer had been removed by the police first. Then she'd turn around and decide if she was going to drop the wine off.

If she did, that was all she would do.

But as the spherical light came into view, she could see there was a row of five cars parked in front of the open gates. Three of them were police patrol vehicles.

Leah slowed right down and the car behind her beeped again. She put her foot down. What was going on in there?

By the time she'd collected herself she realised she hadn't looked out for the deer. After the sharp bend she indicated right, and the other car surged past her. This was the stretch of road where she'd had the near miss with the motorbike. She turned in the yard of the pig farm and headed back.

Rounding the bend again, she scanned the edge of the wall for signs of the deer. It was still there and from the new position of its body it looked like other cars might have struck it since. Why hadn't the police removed it? Perhaps they'd only just turned up. But surely all those cars weren't necessary.

Leah felt a low tremor of dread. She glanced in her rear-view. No traffic behind her. Slowing the car, she peered through the open gates. Two uniformed officers were standing in the gravel courtyard. The yellow front door was wide open, but she couldn't see what was going on in the gloom beyond.

She had to stop. Find out exactly what had happened between now and when she'd left the house eight hours before.

Leah pulled the Vauxhall over, parked in front of the other cars and got out to talk to the officers.

Chapter Nine

As she approached the gates one of the officers was just stretching a piece of yellow striped crime scene tape across it. 'Excuse me...'

The officer frowned. He looked to be no older than late teens, particularly because of the cluster of acne on his cheeks and chin.

'What's happening here?'

He didn't reply but turned in the direction of the other older officer, who strutted straight-legged and noisily across the gravel. Leah put him in his late twenties, and he had the squat physique of a rugby player.

'You shouldn't be stopping here.' The older officer shot at glance at where her blue Vauxhall was parked.

'Can you tell me what's happened?'

'This is a crime scene. Please get back in your vehicle.'

'I'm a neighbour.'

The older officer's expression was set stern. 'Your car is a hazard. Move it, please.'

'Has something happened to the owner?'

He waved her away with a black-gloved hand. 'I'm not at liberty to say.'

'I was in this house late last night. Tell me what's happened.'

The hostility left the older officer's expression. 'OK. Just wait there one moment. Last night?'

She nodded.

'You're a friend of the owner?'

'Not really. My car hit a deer and I used their phone…'

The officer stepped away to have a conversation on his radio.

The younger officer regarded her vacantly.

'Yes. Just pulled up here. OK. I'll let her know.' The older officer moved back to the tape. 'DI Byrne is coming down to speak with you now.'

Leah nodded, already dreading being told the reason for so many officers being on the scene. She remembered the bottle of red wine she'd left on the passenger seat.

Cars hissed by and she felt the fine spray of last night's rain against the back of her legs. She squinted past the two sentries to the open door of the house. The beige umbrella she'd borrowed was still leaning against the left-hand side of the doorway. The dark blue car was still parked in the driveway but the silver one wasn't.

Less than a minute later a tall, slender woman with red hair shorn tight to her head walked out of the house and picked her way across the courtyard in a pair of short black heels. Her legs were clad in grey denim and she clutched her green parka to her as the wind picked up. She made eye contact with Leah long before she reached her, intently gauging her as she approached the gates.

'I'm DI Helen Byrne.' She didn't extend her hand.

'Leah Talbot.'

The wind rippled the yellow tape between them.

'You live close by?'

'That's right.'

'And you visited this property last night?'

'Yes.' Leah detected a vague Irish accent and already felt intimidated by the woman's pale blue gaze. 'I didn't intend to. My car hit a deer just down there.' She pointed to where the animal still lay. 'I knocked on this door because it was the closest and used their telephone.'

'Your car was badly damaged?'

'It had to be towed.'

Byrne's eyes darted. 'What time was this?'

'Between eleven and twelve.'

Byrne blinked, as she absorbed that.

'Can you tell me what's happened?'

Byrne sucked on her lip. 'The owner of the property has been murdered.'

Leah felt her stomach drop. A lorry rumbled by loudly behind her and seemed to take a long time to pass.

'And they were fine when you left?'

'I borrowed an umbrella while I waited for the pickup. That's it there.' Leah pointed, stunned.

But Byrne didn't turn to look at it, maintaining eye contact with Leah. 'So you were picked up soon after?'

'Yes. By the AA.'

'But you live close by.'

'I know but my car needed to be towed because the wheel arch was crushed.' Sounded like she was a suspect. Her circulation surged. 'The AA guy dropped me off. Phone and ask.'

'OK. We can do that. You went home immediately afterwards?'

'Yes.'

'Somebody waiting for you there?'

'Yes. My husband.' She hadn't called Elliot that for a while. 'At least, he came in a little after me.'

Byrne nodded gently, her eyes narrowed. 'How long after?'

Leah couldn't believe what she was suddenly in the middle of. 'Can I get off the road?'

DI Byrne didn't step back. 'In a moment. Just try to remember the last thing she said to you before you left.'

Another heavy vehicle trundled by but Leah knew she hadn't misheard. 'Who?'

Impatience registered on Byrne's face. 'Alice Booth. The woman who lived here.'

Chapter Ten

Nine hours earlier

B lood flowed from Tate's blue surgically gloved hands and swirled down the plughole of Alice Booth's en suite sink. She lay on the bed behind him, her overfed dog, Sheila, trying to climb up to the mattress to see her but failing to raise itself on its stumpy legs.

Alice had been dead for around forty minutes and he wanted to make sure he left only her body for discovery. The water ran pink then clear and he dried his rubber-clad hands in the fluffy marine towel beside the sink. Tate walked back into the bedroom and, even though she was propped up on the pillows, it appeared Alice was staring straight at him out of a red mask. There was no hint of life in her dull gaze, however.

He whistled sharply. 'Come on, Sheila. Away from there.'

The dog obeyed and lolloped over to where he was standing.

'Nothing else to see here now. Come on.' He led the animal to the door. He would lock it shut behind him. There would be no vestige of dignity if the basset hound did manage to get to her wounds.

Three firm knocks on the front door.

He froze. 'Stay,' he cautioned Sheila and then padded lightly over to the window. He couldn't turn off the light; that would attract the caller's attention. Instead he peeked through the plantation blind into the courtyard below. There was a woman standing there.

He ducked back again. As far as he knew, Alice Booth had no friends. Perhaps it was a neighbour. There were no properties nearby though.

She knocked again.

He took another look. Longer this time. The woman turned to survey the courtyard. She seemed nervous. Why was she calling this late? But as she shifted back her profile was familiar to him. He caught his breath. It seemed too much of a coincidence. Forley was a small village though.

He could so easily wait for her to leave. Give her the five minutes it would take him to finish cleaning up and probably find her gone when he slipped out. Instead, however, he slipped off his left glove as he hurried to the bedroom door.

Sheila obediently followed him and he pulled the handle with his gloved right hand and made sure it was firmly shut. He checked himself in the full-length mirror on the landing. No blood spatters on his face or clothes. Then he headed down the stairs to the hall and used his gloved hand to unlock it. He swung it wide and as it opened inwards, deftly slipping off the remaining glove and tucking both into his back pocket.

He waited while the woman explained why she was on Alice Booth's doorstep. It was immediately clear she didn't recognise him.

Tate invited her in to use the phone. He couldn't make her walk all the way back to Forley, and he knew there was nowhere else nearby. Again, he considered it would have been easy to leave her outside but knew she was Leah Talbot before she gave her name.

He told her his was Martin Tate. It was the name he'd used for the past seven months.

She'd killed something that night. Not in a calculated fashion as he had but she had blood all over her hand.

He told her she could clean herself in the downstairs bathroom and waited for her outside. He picked up the phone. Had to remember to clean that before he left.

As he listened to the water flow, he considered how he'd been washing blood from his fingers only moments before. Where was the dog? He looked around for it. Had it followed him downstairs?

Leah Talbot came out of the bathroom but looked very pale. He pretended to be finishing a call to the police. Now he didn't have to go through the performance of speaking to a dead line.

He waited patiently as she left a message for her husband. How ridiculous that Elliot was so unreachable on Valentine's night. There was clearly something wrong at home. He offered her a seat but she seemed nervous. It was understandable but when Sheila came down the stairs that seemed to reassure her. Perfect timing, pooch.

She almost passed out but he caught her. Touched Leah Talbot for the first time. Felt the solidity of her radius and ulna and the warmth of the flesh around them through the sleeve of her black jumper. Tate escorted her to the kitchen where Alice Booth's dinner was sitting on the breakfast bar. He was just considering how she would react if Leah realised it was stone cold. He *had* just told her he was in the middle of dinner. But that became academic when she fainted.

He regarded Leah lying on her side at his feet, pocketed Alice Booth's phone handset and then slipped his gloves back on. He was about to lift her but paused, pulled out a stool from the kitchen bar and seated himself. He took a few minutes to take in her oblivious expression. She'd had a real ordeal by the sound of it. She frowned but there was no further reaction.

Tate fished her phone out of her bag and plugged it in to charge. Ten minutes later, he replaced it, scooped her up and carried her into Alice's lounge, delicately settling her into one of the armchairs before putting her handbag on the coffee table.

He brushed her damp hair from her face and then gently kissed her on the lips.

Her lips felt cold but tasted of whatever berry chapstick she was wearing. He could detect another aroma around her – the gamey scent of the animal she'd killed. He lifted her hands and examined them. They were warm and pristine now but her sleeve felt damp.

Tate dropped into the armchair opposite and scrutinised Leah Talbot but her head lolled forward and her chin dropped to her chest. He stood, took her face in his hands and repositioned it carefully against the headrest. He resisted kissing her a second time and chided himself for his first infraction. He wouldn't take advantage again.

He took out the phone handset and sat down and it was fortunate he did because at that moment she started to come round. He quickly removed the gloves and slipped them into his front pocket. When she awoke properly, he reassured her and then went into the kitchen.

He'd already gone through Alice Booth's purse on the dresser. He slipped on one glove and used his clad hand to open it again. He found her AA card and called them using her membership number. While he did so he opened and closed some cupboards and found a few bottles of booze. He located a glass and poured Leah a brandy. He pocketed the glove and took the drink into the lounge.

Clean the phone, clean the glass.

The brandy went to her head. Small wonder. She had plenty of adrenaline to zip it around her. She almost fell again and something happened. Something he really hadn't expected. They kissed, only a few minutes after he'd tasted her mouth for the first time. She clearly needed to be comforted after her ordeal, but it made her suddenly nervous of him.

And now she wanted to leave. He'd overstepped the mark and he didn't want to make the situation any more uncomfortable for her. He offered the umbrella. Told her she could drop it back to him to test her reaction.

She rejected it but as she marched away he wondered if she wanted to come back. Even though he would be far from Alice Booth's house when she did.

He watched her umbrella cross the courtyard in the pouring rain to the gates and closed the front door. Then he went back upstairs and turned out the light in Alice's room. He watched Leah through the plantation blinds. She was standing outside the open gates talking to the driver.

He would come back later. Finish cleaning up. But now he headed downstairs to his own car. Once Leah Talbot had been taken to the scene of her accident further down the road, he would follow the breakdown truck to wherever it took her.

She'd already told him which road she lived in and even at which number. But now she could show him exactly where.

Chapter Eleven

'Is this your car?' DI Byrne ducked under the crime scene tape and gestured towards the vehicle.

Leah nodded.

'The one you were in last night?' Byrne squinted as she examined it.

'No. I told you, mine had to be towed. This is my husband's.'

'Let's get in. We'll take a statement from you right away about this Martin Tate, while everything's still fresh in your head.'

Leah walked unsteadily along the thin grass verge to the car, extending her arms for balance as another heavy vehicle wafted noisily by. Was Martin Tate a relative of the woman who had been murdered? She recalled the photos on the dresser in the lounge. She hadn't seen his face in any of them. Had she really spent half an hour with the man who had killed her?

She opened the driver's door and got in. DI Byrne was

shouting back at somebody coming out of the gates. Leah pulled the door closed, the din of the road muffled so her own thoughts could roar.

The kiss. That was all she was remembering now. The heat of his mouth and how she'd wanted to remain against it. How could the man who had been so kind to her be a killer? He'd called the police. And the breakdown people. There had to be an explanation. He couldn't have murdered somebody. If he had, why would he have opened the door to her?

But if it wasn't his house, why his presence so late? He'd acted the whole time as if it were his home. He hadn't mentioned anyone else living there. There had been no sign of a woman. Maybe DI Byrne had got her facts wrong.

But there was obviously a body. A woman. Leah shuddered. Had she really been dead the whole time Leah had been there? She recalled passing out and waking in the lounge. What had happened during that time? Leah remembered the brandy he gave her. Had it been drugged? If she hadn't insisted on leaving would she have passed out and become another victim? But she'd been fine when she'd got home. Shaken but certainly not able to sleep until a good few hours after Elliot had gone to bed and her phone had finished charging.

The passenger door abruptly opened, letting in the noise of the road again. DI Byrne picked up the bottle of wine that was resting in the seat and dropped into it.

Leah turned as the rear passenger door opened too. A blonde-bearded plain-clothes officer wearing a black Superdry rain jacket slid along the seat.

'This is Sergeant Fitch.' Byrne cast her eyes to the back seat. 'He's going to take your statement.' She examined the wine label momentarily, rested it carefully on its side on the dash and pulled her door closed.

Fitch did the same as Leah turned to take him in properly. He looked to be in his thirties and his fair hair had receded leaving only a tuft on his forehead. He nodded at Leah but said nothing. Leaning back, he pulled a tablet out of his pocket.

'Are you OK?' Byrne squinted at her, but the expression was devoid of concern.

Leah could already feel blood surging through her cheeks. 'I'm fine … just … shocked, I suppose.'

'Not as shocked as Ms Booth's cleaner.' The detective's Irish accent seemed suddenly strident.

'Did she find her?'

Byrne nodded, rubbed her eyes. 'Early this morning. Alice Booth was supposed to be going on holiday. Red-eye flight. Cleaner had the key and didn't expect to find her in.'

'Where was she found?'

Byrne ignored Leah's question and turned to Fitch. 'Ready?'

Fitch nodded at his tablet.

Byrne asked Leah about her collision with the deer again and her movements preceding it. Leah gave her as many details as possible.

Byrne looked straight ahead the whole time she interviewed Leah. 'So you walked along this main road because you knew the house was here?'

'Not really. I mean, I drive by the house all the time, but

it was only when I saw the outside light on that I remembered it was there.'

'It's an electric gate. Did you ring the buzzer outside?'

'No. The gate was open. There were two cars parked at the front.'

'Two cars?'

'One dark blue and one silver.'

'You didn't notice the number or the make of the silver car?' But Byrne's tone said she already knew the answer.

'No. The silver car was smaller than the blue car though. I crossed the courtyard and knocked on the front door.'

Byrne waited a moment while Fitch tapped his screen.

'And a man answered the door?'

'Yes.'

'Describe him.

Leah did, as well as she could. Then she explained how he'd let her wash her hands before he phoned the police.

'Did you hear that conversation?'

'I was in the washroom at the time. Caught the end of it as I came out. He was just giving them the address.'

'So he could have been talking to anyone … or nobody?'

Leah nodded at Byrne. Had it been a performance?

'There was no call to us about this address, a deer or anything else last night.'

'But he called the breakdown service and they turned up. Why would he do that?'

'Indeed. Which breakdown service?'

'Mine. The AA. He used his membership to call but the pickup driver then took my details.'

'We'll check into that. Fitch, make a note.'

Fitch's rain jacket hissed as he nodded his head.

'He let me call my husband. He was out so I had to leave a message on his mobile. Then he invited me in to wait but I didn't feel comfortable.'

'Why not?'

It was a good question. She recalled feeling uneasy being in the house when nobody knew she was there. 'Then his ... *her* dog came down the stairs and I petted it.'

'And that made you feel more comfortable?'

Leah thought about it and nodded.

'You're a dog person?'

'Yes. Don't own one though. My husband is allergic. At least, that's what he tells me.'

'Where is your husband now? Does he know you're here?'

Leah wondered how to answer.

Chapter Twelve

'He's out on a run.' It was the truth but not a response to the second part of the question.

DI Byrne still didn't turn to look at her but remined focused on the Saturday traffic. 'So why did you come back here?'

Leah reluctantly glanced at the bottle of wine on the dash. 'I came to check the deer had been moved but it's still there.'

Byrne waited for her to elaborate.

'Then I saw the police cars outside, so I turned around and came back.'

'OK. So the dog made you feel more comfortable. What happened then?'

'He led me into the kitchen but I was starting to feel faint at that point. I have low blood pressure and I think I was still in shock.'

'Why would he take you there?'

'It was the nearest room, I suppose. And he was in the middle of eating.'

Byrne swivelled to her, eyebrow raised. 'He ate while you waited?'

'No. But I saw the meal on the breakfast bar.' Leah wondered if he'd cooked for himself after he'd killed Alice Booth. Or had that been her meal? And her glass of wine? She'd brought a bottle of red as a gift because she'd thought it had been his.

'Was he acting strangely? On edge?'

'No. He seemed very relaxed. Very much at home.' Leah could hear Fitch tapping away at his tablet.

'What did you talk about while you waited in the kitchen?'

'There was no conversation because at that point I passed out.'

Byrne raised her other eyebrow. 'You collapsed?'

'I assume so. When I woke up, I was sitting in an armchair in the lounge.'

'He carried you there?'

A cold current passed across Leah's shoulders as she imagined him doing so. What else could he have done while she'd been unconscious?

'How long were you out?'

'Only a few minutes.'

'You're sure?'

Leah wasn't. She frowned hard. Remembered how he'd been sat opposite her when she'd opened her eyes. 'It must have been.' She tried to recall the next time she'd checked her watch. Had it been when she'd got home? 'He gave me a brandy to revive me.'

'Brandy?'

'I didn't want it. I don't usually drink spirits.'

'But you took it?' Byrne guessed.

'Yes.'

'Make a note,' she told Fitch. 'So you were feeling a lot more comfortable by then?'

'No, but he put it in my hand right after he called the AA.'

'So it would have been rude to refuse?'

Fitch's tapping halted, as if he were waiting for her answer as well.

'It did steady my nerves.'

'And you felt OK afterwards, no feelings of drowsiness?'

Looked like Byrne was already entertaining similar thoughts to her. 'No. I was a little dizzy. He offered to call me an ambulance. I was fine after that though.' But Leah was dreading being pressed further.

'But, as far as you were concerned, he was the homeowner?'

'Yes.'

Byrne turned her attention front again, but her gaze was on the bottle. 'So what's this for?'

Leah frowned but Byrne's attention was on the wine. 'It's the weekend.'

'Have you just bought it then?'

She obviously hadn't. Not during this trip. 'No. It's my husband's.' She sounded too defensive.

'That's right. It's his car.'

Leah waited to be asked why he would have a full bottle of wine in his car first thing in the morning, but Byrne's eyes darted as she turned something over in her head.

'What did you talk about while you waited for the pickup to arrive?'

'It arrived quickly after.'

'But you must have had some conversation during that time.'

'He went out into the kitchen to get the brandy and to make the call.'

'So you had no other discussions?'

'Not really.' But now was the time to tell them what really happened. 'At that point, I told him I wanted to wait for the pickup outside.' He'd kissed *her*, hadn't he?

Fitch's fingers drummed on the tablet.

'Why did you want to wait outside?'

'I still felt a bit dizzy but I put that down to my low blood pressure. I still wasn't feeling comfortable waiting there though, so I got up to leave.' But Leah wasn't giving them the real reason.

'What did he say?'

'He tried to get me to stay but I said I wanted to go. He told me it was raining and that I could borrow an umbrella.'

'And you did?'

'Yes. The one on the doorstep.'

But Byrne still didn't seem interested in it. 'So you went out of a warm and dry house into the rain?'

'I felt I'd overstayed my welcome.'

'Did he give you that impression?'

'Not at all. It was … my decision.'

64

'And that was that?'

'Yes. I thanked him and then walked to the gate. It was tipping down but then the pickup arrived.'

'That was double quick time then.' Byrne turned to her again. 'How long was the time between him calling and the pickup arriving?'

'Five, ten minutes. I expect you can check that.'

'Yes.' Byrne cast her eyes briefly to Fitch. 'We can.'

Chapter Thirteen

L eah tried not to swallow as DI Byrne considered her story.

'So that was the last you saw of him?'

'Yes,' Leah answered without hesitation, glad to have passed the part of the account she didn't want to relay. She'd been attracted to a complete stranger, a man who had very probably murdered Alice Booth. Did that need to go on record? If she admitted to it, might Elliot find out? But another horrible thought overrode it. 'I did tell him where I live.'

Byrne registered alarm. 'Why would you do that?'

'For the police. Because I thought he was a neighbour. I believed he lived in that house,' she replied, exasperated.

'At what point was this?'

'I gave him my door number as I left.'

Byrne puffed her cheeks.

'To give to the police when they arrived. I thought they'd want to speak to me about the deer.'

Byrne's face was stern. 'Do you have any children?'

'No.'

'Just your husband at home then? When he finishes his run?'

'Yes.' Leah's temple started pounding. 'Do you think we're in danger?'

Byrne pursed her lips but said nothing.

It wasn't the reaction Leah wanted.

'Can you contact your husband?'

'He should have his phone with him.' Leah took out hers. 'I can call him now.'

'You'd better.'

She speed-dialled his number but got his answering service. He rarely picked up the phone to her nowadays. Leah imagined him taking out his phone, looking at her number and then pocketing it again. 'Elliot. It's me. I'm with the police. Something's happened. Please, please call me as soon as you get this message.'

'Tell him not to go home.' Byrne prompted.

'Don't go back to the house. Go to the café. Wait for me there. Just do this and call me straight away.' She hesitated, looked at Byrne for further advice but the detective just nodded. She hung up. 'I've got to get back.'

'Fitch will go with you. OK?' She shot a glance at the officer and he nodded once. 'Just for safety. Did the man at the house extract this information from you?'

'No.' That was correct. She'd volunteered her address. Could she feel any more foolish?

'There's nothing else you've neglected to mention?'

But Leah was desperate to leave. 'No.'

Byrne didn't seem convinced. 'I appreciate you're distressed but I'd like you to have a long think about every detail of your visit here.'

'Yes. I will. I'd like to go now though.' Or was she also eager to finish the conversation?

'Fitch, take your car.'

'That's fine. We'll go in this one.'

'It's parked just behind us.' Fitch reassured her. 'I can get us there faster.'

'OK.' Leah wondered why but didn't want to waste time arguing about it. She got out of the car.

The two officers quickly followed.

'Take a good look around.' Byrne told Fitch then met Leah's eye. 'Don't worry. I'm sure he's far away from here by now.'

But Leah caught the worry in the DI's glance to her fellow officer.

'This one.' Fitch gestured at an unmarked car parked in front of the patrol vehicles. It was a tan Audi.

The locks shot and Leah opened the door. What time would Elliot get back from his run? She jumped into the passenger seat and Fitch's door slammed the same time as hers.

He started the engine. 'Forley?'

'Yes.'

'My sister lives here.' Fitch pulled out into the traffic and both lanes halted and honked as he u-turned and accelerated to the lights.

'Seat belt.' He nodded at Leah, even though he wasn't wearing his.

She pulled it across her and willed the lights to stay on green as they reached them.

They did and Fitch shot through. 'Left at the roundabout, yeah?'

Leah nodded. She tried calling Elliot again but still got his answering service.

'Where's this café you told him to wait at?'

'Top of Minster Street. Langtry's.'

'I'll drop you there.'

'No. I'm coming with you.'

'But your husband might have stopped off there.'

'No he won't have. He doesn't do anything I ask him to.'

Fitch nodded once, turned at the roundabout and sped towards the crossroads that would take them to the high street.

Chapter Fourteen

Nine hours earlier

Tate waited for the breakdown truck to pass Alice Booth's house with Leah Talbot's little green Fiat hitched to the back before opening the gates, pulling out of the driveway and following a few moments later in his silver Nissan. He'd chosen the vehicle because it was nondescript but even though it was dark, he had to be careful about which road he used to enter Forley. There were plenty of lights and cameras in the high street.

He let them turn left but went straight on at the roundabout and followed the long one-way system until he was passing the carefully manicured bowling green before turning left himself and driving down Minster Street. He slowed, not wanting to meet them coming the other way.

He took in the driveway of each house, looking for the breakdown vehicle, but as he rounded the slight bend, saw it on his right. It was parked up at the front with its headlights on. Leah Talbot was still sitting in the passenger seat. He kept his eyes front as he passed and then pulled his Nissan into a space on the left about thirty yards further on.

Switching off the engine he kept an eye on the truck in the side mirror. She was probably signing a digital screen for her car. Seconds later, she emerged from her door and he heard her thank the driver before she walked up the driveway to her house. The driver took a minute or so tapping some details into his handset and then consulting his GPS before he took off with the damaged car.

Tate waited for the rear headlights to fade and then got out of the car, locked it and crossed the road. He passed the low hedge at the front of the house and could see light shining through the leaves. He paused briefly at the driveway. There was a white square illuminating the edges of the garage door and a weak light in the hallway window.

He could see a tall wooden door at the side and assumed he could get to the back that way, but it might be locked. His eyes shifted to the neighbouring houses. The one on the left was in darkness but there were lights on in the top windows of the one on the right. Maybe there was a way in at the rear that would allow him to operate in the dark.

He walked back the way he'd come. He hadn't seen any roads off Minster Street as he'd driven in so he would check in the opposite direction. He counted the front doors he passed and, sixty paces later, came to a side street on his right and headed down it, looking for CCTV cameras but seeing none.

To his right was an overgrown alleyway. That had to run

behind the houses on Minster Street. There were no lights down there. Even better. He resisted the temptation to use the torch on his phone and traversed the brambles and counted the back gates until he came to the one he wanted. Then he reached in his pocket, pulled out a fresh pair of surgical gloves and slipped them on.

He put his hand on the metal ring and tried to twist it. Locked? No, it was just stiff. With a little more force it rotated, and he used his shoulder to nudge it open. He didn't push it all the way but waited, in case anyone had heard and was looking out of their back windows.

A duck quacked behind him and he turned. Beyond the overgrown reeds there was a stream and a group of the birds were curled up on the bank asleep, heads tucked under their wings. Only one of them seemed agitated by his presence.

He counted to twenty and then pushed the gate half open. It was enough space for him to slip through, but he scanned the overgrown lawn ahead first. It was dimly lit by a light on in the kitchen. There was nobody in the room. Didn't she say her husband, Elliot, hadn't been home? That had been when she'd first arrived at Alice Booth's though. Maybe he was back now. But he couldn't see any sign of him. His eyes tilted up to the window above. Another light was on there and one next door to the left too.

He could cross the lawn area in darkness if he stuck to the right edge of it. He entered the garden, trod lightly along the flower bed and stood halfway across the long, wet grass behind some buddleia branches. The window above was frosted. Had to be the bathroom. He could make out a shelf containing bottles and a dark cabinet at the back. His eyes darted quickly left to the lit window next door. Orange curtains were drawn there. Nobody investigating his opening of the gate.

When he was sure the kitchen was empty, he strode to the window to look through into the house. It would mean he would momentarily be standing in the light, but he needed to see the space where she lived. Just quickly. But when he got to the pane, he saw his reflection there.

Tate didn't have a mirror at home. Didn't like to catch himself looking back. It was because, since he'd been in his mid-twenties, he'd no longer seen himself as a person. He just saw components: a pair of eyes connected to a brain that was connected to a stem that was connected to a body. Individual pieces slotted together into a whole that he was no longer fooled into seeing.

He didn't know why it had happened. There had been no trigger event that he could pinpoint. He'd lost all the friends he had then because he saw them in the same way. And he'd felt the same about the girls he'd once been so intrigued by. Realised that they were built differently but only slightly differently, crudely customised with curves and eyelashes and breasts to distract him from so effortlessly deconstructing them.

But Leah had sparked something else. Something nostalgic. When he'd first laid eyes on her he'd not just seen a physical assembly. He'd seen her as a whole.

He returned his attention to the bathroom. Was Leah Talbot up there alone, brushing her teeth before bed? He recalled how her lips had tasted when he'd kissed her as she sat unconscious in the chair and then later when they'd briefly responded.

A pink shape flitted past the window. He kept his gaze fixed there until it appeared again. Looked like Leah had got undressed. He looked down at his feet. Now he felt uncomfortable. He wasn't a Peeping Tom. Why was he risking himself like this? He returned his eyes to the window.

A few seconds later he could hear the low hiss of water. Thirty feet away, she was standing under the jets. He imagined her eyes closed against their intensity, that moment that he always enjoyed alone when the droplets ran down his skin and he felt like an entity again.

He could feel the warmth flowing down to her feet and trickling away through the plughole, see the orange shapes in her eyelids closed against the firm pressure of the water while briefly no breath was being drawn in through the three holes of her face.

She was washing away the events of the night. That raw animal aroma that had been about her. She'd be soaping her hands again now. Moving the palms harshly against each other even though they were already clean. Was she thinking about him? Was his face inside her skull? A sensation crept over him again, one he had struggled to identify but that felt familiar.

But its presence had been low-key before now. Had been nagging at him for the past few days. Maybe he should let it overcome him.

The frosted window started to steam up, blurring the shapes of what he could see.

Chapter Fifteen

'Turn here.' Leah indicated the right turning down Minster Street and realised how breathless she sounded.

Fitch complied. 'Can you see your husband there?' He squinted at Langtry's on the left.

Leah surveyed the people sitting in the conservatory at the front of the building. No Elliot.

Fitch parked up in front of the café. 'Better get out and check.'

Leah undid her seat belt. 'Please, wait for me.'

'I can't get into the house without you,' he said placatingly.

Leah opened her door, trotted up the path to the café and leaned through the entrance. The interior was busy but there was no sign of Elliot at the tables or counter. Had he gone home?

'OK. Where's your place?' Fitch asked as soon as she slid back into the passenger seat.

77

'About halfway up and on the left.'

Fitch accelerated hard but had to stop for a car pulling out of a driveway. 'Come on.' He pulled to the side and waved them on.

She recognised her neighbour's face glowering from the other car but his expression changed when he recognised Leah sitting beside the police officer.

Fitch picked up speed again and shot around the curve.

'Number thirty-three. Just park here.' Leah was almost out of the car before it stopped.

'Wait. Let me go in first.' Fitch closed his door, eyes on the front of the house.

Leah waited for him to enter their driveway. His eyes briefly shot to the bushes around the tall grass of the small front lawn before he focused on the front door.

Leah followed him and he didn't object.

'Any security system?'

'No.' Nobody had a burglar alarm in Forley. There were few thefts. The village had been targeted by a gang who had robbed a few properties during the Solstice carnival but that had been over three years ago.

Fitch reached the front door. 'Let me have your key then.' He turned, fingers outstretched.

Leah pulled the keys from her bag and held up the main one before handing them to him.

Fitch took them and was about to insert the key into the lock when he paused. He pushed on the door and was able to nudge it slightly inwards. He turned to Leah again, a frown on his face.

Had she forgotten to pull the front door closed? No, she'd left via the back. Had Elliot left it open on his way out?

Fitch pushed the door so it swung half in and then leaned inside and examined the lock. 'It's on the latch. Was that you?'

'No.'

'Your husband?'

Her shoulders bristled cold. 'I don't know.'

'Elliot, you said?'

Leah nodded.

'Elliot!' Fitch called out.

No response.

Fitch held out his palm. 'Just wait here.' He stepped over the threshold.

Leah immediately moved to the front door and watched him pause at the foot of the stairs.

'Mr Talbot!' He shouted up them, louder.

Still no reply.

Leah turned and looked back down the driveway, hoping to see a sweaty Elliot trotting up it. Maybe he would wait at Langtry's.

'Anybody home?' Fitch yelled.

Nobody answered.

Perhaps he'd left the door on the latch because he didn't think she'd be going out. She'd only decided to drive to the house after he'd left. There was no reason to panic. She entered the hallway.

Fitch turned to her. 'Stay outside, please.'

Leah took a step back but remained in the hall.

'I'll check upstairs first.' Fitch swiftly climbed.

Leah heard him moving about up there. Doors opening, floorboards creaking and then his return along the landing before he descended again.

'Not up here. I thought you said nobody else lived here with you.'

'They don't.' But she knew why Fitch was asking. 'Just the two of us.'

'OK.' Fitch had reached the bottom of the stairs and nodded, awkwardly. He'd obviously seen unmade beds in both rooms. 'I'll just check the downstairs.' He changed the subject quickly.

'He must still be out. Shall I try him again?' She took her phone from her handbag.

Fitch nodded again and turned to the closed doors down the hallway.

A rattle.

Both of them froze. It had come from the kitchen.

'Mr Talbot?' Fitch gestured for her to stay back.

It came again, louder this time.

If it was Elliot, why wasn't he answering? Maybe he'd only just come back and still had his earbuds in.

Fitch seemed nervous and didn't proceed further.

'Elliot!' Leah called now.

They both waited. No sound.

'What's going on?'

Leah turned to find Elliot standing behind her, face flushed red.

'Why did you ask me to go to the café?'

Leah shushed him and turned back to Fitch.

He gestured for quiet and they waited for the sound in the kitchen to come again.

Chapter Sixteen

'Who's this?' Elliot nodded at Fitch.

'The police.' Leah hissed. 'Wait.'

Fitch took a couple of paces towards the kitchen but halted when the same noise came again.

Leah thought the rattle was familiar, but it was accompanied by a series of thuds.

Elliot joined Leah but his expression had frozen. He exchanged a look with her but didn't speak.

Fitch put his hand on the kitchen door and pushed it inwards.

From over his shoulder, Leah could see into most of the room. It looked empty, but the sound intensified. The acoustics said it was definitely inside.

Fitch pushed the door open all the way and moved across the wooden floor tiles towards the French doors.

Elliot crept past Leah and was the first to the doorway but hesitated there as the officer moved tentatively on.

Fitch froze, his head directed downward. 'Looks like you've got a visitor.'

Leah slid past Elliot in the doorway and joined Fitch, her gaze following his.

There was a duck, a green-necked drake, standing stock still by the French doors. It eyed them both with a shiny black eye.

Leah's shoulders dropped and she breathed again.

'How the hell did that get in here?' Elliot said from behind her.

Fitch turned to them. 'It's not a pet then?'

'There's more ducks in Forley than people. It must have come in through the open front door.' Leah was thinking out loud.

The duck turned back to the chain hanging beside the vertical blinds and tugged it with its beak. It rattled and the action knocked the blinds against the glass.

'Is this what the emergency is?' Elliot addressed them both.

Leah turned to him. 'Did you leave the door on the latch?'

'No,' he immediately answered. 'I ... don't think so anyway.'

Leah sighed.

'So you called the police because you heard that in here?'

She exchanged a look with Fitch and shook her head. 'There's a bit more to it than that.'

Fitch crouched to the animal. 'Shall we open the door

and let this fella out then? I think he's had more of a fright than us.'

Leah could see the dark wet droppings at the base of the door. 'Key's here.' She took it from a pot on the dresser and handed it to him.

'I'll have a check around outside as well.' He unlocked the door and shooed the duck. It scuttled out, flapped its wings and flew ten feet before resting again in the middle of the overgrown back lawn.

'What's been going on?' Elliot asked as soon as Fitch had followed it into the garden.

But Leah's focus was on the back gate at the bottom. It looked like it was closed tight, and, although she felt embarrassed that the grass was almost up to the officer's thighs, it didn't look as if anyone had recently crossed the lawn.

Fitch scanned the area and the duck scampered into the overgrown buddleia patch at the left of the garden. The officer reached the gate, opened it and looked up and down the alleyway that ran behind the houses.

'Are you OK?' Elliot knew she didn't scare easily.

She didn't turn to him but nodded as she waited for Fitch to pull the gate closed. 'Somebody's been murdered.'

There was a pause before Elliot responded. 'What?'

Leah turned to face him. 'When I had my accident last night I stopped at a house on Plough Lane. When I couldn't get a response from you, a man there helped me.'

Elliot's eyes dipped to the floor.

Leah folded her arms. 'I went back this morning to thank him and there were police cars outside.'

Elliot met her gaze again. 'He's dead?' He asked incredulously.

'No. A woman lived there. *She's* dead. I think the man who opened the door to me, who said his name was Martin Tate, was the one who killed her.'

Elliot's eyes widened as he allowed that to sink in.

'He told me he'd called the police about the deer so I told him where we live so they could contact me. That's why the police officer escorted me back.'

Elliot shook his head. 'Jesus.' His body language said he was about to hug her.

But even though she needed it, Leah kept her arms tight to her chest.

Fitch walked back through the French doors. 'I don't think anybody has been in the back.' He addressed Elliot. 'That front door wasn't forced. You really can't recall if it was you that left it on the latch?'

Elliot blinked as he attempted to remember.

'Do you generally put it on the latch?'

'Sometimes. Not often.' Elliot shook his head.

'Even if it was you, somebody could have come in though.' Leah tried to calculate how long she'd been absent. Just over half an hour? Maybe longer?

'Yes, but I think it was likely to be just our little visitor in the garden.' Fitch was looking back through the doors again.

Leah hoped he was right.

'I'll check upstairs.' Elliot turned to the door.

'I've been up but it won't hurt to double check all the

rooms. You'd know if anything has been taken or disturbed. I'll wait here while you do that. Take your time.'

Elliot nodded and trotted out.

But Leah didn't feel reassured. It stood to reason that Martin Tate would have fled. But as she watched the duck flutter upwards and onto the top of the back garden wall, she recalled that the front door hadn't been wide open when they'd arrived at the house.

Maybe it had blown almost shut after the duck had wandered in.

Chapter Seventeen

E lliot came down the stairs. 'All fine by the looks of it.'
Fitch was waiting with Leah in the hallway. 'OK.
Good.'

'You checked the windows?' Leah asked him.

'Yep.' Elliot sounded like he hadn't but nodded to indicate he had.

'Should I check?' She met his eye.

'I confirmed that when I went up.' Fitch stepped in. 'I'll get back to the crime scene now but maybe you should both look around and reassure yourselves that everything's as it should be.'

Elliot reached the bottom of the stairs. 'Should we really stay here?'

Leah realised that Elliot was as spooked as her.

'That's your call.' Fitch zipped up his jacket and then took in their expressions. 'If you can't remember leaving the door on the latch...'

Elliot shook his head. 'No. I don't. Maybe we should stay somewhere else tonight.'

'OK. Give me a number I can reach you on.' Fitch turned to Leah. 'I'll get an officer to drive your car back over later today.'

Later today? Did they need to examine it because she was a suspect? Was that why Fitch had insisted on bringing her home in his car?

'Is there anything inside it you need? Aside from that bottle of wine?' Fitch quipped.

'Bottle of wine?' Elliot repeated.

But Leah was imagining officers fingerprinting Elliot's car. 'No. We'll need the car back soon though, if we have to drive somewhere.'

'Of course. Give me the keys and your phone number and I'll let you know as soon as someone's on their way.'

She did, Fitch tapped the number into his phone and then sent her his. 'You two going to be OK?'

Leah nodded for both of them. 'Just really unnerved by the whole thing.'

'You'll let us know as soon as you catch this guy?' Elliot looked apprehensively out at the driveway.

'I'll keep you in the loop. You'll be here for the next hour?'

Leah nodded.

'OK. I'll be in touch soon. If you see anyone who makes you suspicious, call me straightaway.' He strode quickly back to his car.

Elliot closed the door and made sure it was securely in place. 'I think we should leave as soon as we can.'

'You really think it's necessary?' But Leah had already come to the same conclusion.

'Even if I did leave the door open, this guy knows exactly where you are.'

'Dad won't mind if we both descend on him.' Leah's mother had died in 2018 and she frequently felt guilty about how she'd only seen him at weekends since the funeral. But then she caught the look in Elliot's eye.

'I could go to a friend.' His gaze was on the bannister.

Why had she assumed the situation meant they would go somewhere together?

'I mean, if you'd prefer it if I went with you...'

Leah couldn't tell if the offer was genuine. And she didn't want him accompanying her out of a sense of duty that he'd happily dispensed with for the past couple of years. 'I'll be fine. It'll be good to spend a bit more time with Dad.'

'If you're sure...'

She didn't respond to that.

'I'll throw some things in a bag.' But he remained at the bottom of the stairs.

Had she just turned him down when he was trying to help? Or had he already made his mind up about sleeping at a friend's? 'Will you need your car then? I can always call the breakdown people and find out how long they're going to be with mine.'

'It's fine. Take the Vauxhall when they bring it back.' He still loitered awkwardly.

'How will you get to...?' She realised she had no idea where he'd be going.

'I'll sort something out.'

'If you're sure.' It was like the politeness of strangers and she hated it.

Elliot put his foot on the stair but paused. 'Why did you have a bottle of wine in the car?'

'I took it over as a thank you for helping me.' She didn't meet his eye now.

'Why would he let you into the house if he'd just murdered somebody?'

Leah was still perplexed by that. There had to be an explanation. A reason for his presence that the police were yet to discover. 'We don't know the full story yet. Perhaps he had every right to be there. But there was a meal on the table. He told me it was his. Didn't mention her at all.'

'You went right inside?'

She couldn't blame his disbelief. 'Yes. Everything seemed so normal. There was a dog and the smell of cooking. I didn't think I was doing anything wrong to tell him where we live.'

Elliot filled his lungs and seemed about to say something but checked himself and nodded. 'Looks like you might have had a lucky escape.'

But had she? Leah couldn't tell him what had passed between them.

'I think we should both be ready to leave as soon as the car gets here.'

'You don't have to wait here with me.' But Leah knew what his reaction would be.

'I'll get a few things ready, but I won't be going until

you're in that car.' He didn't wait for her response but headed upstairs.

Leah walked back into the kitchen and tried the back door. Bolted with no signs of tampering. She locked the French doors and then methodically checked the windows.

Her phone buzzed and she took it from her handbag. It was a text message from an unknown number. Leah opened it.

We need to talk about our kiss last night. Can I see you again?

Chapter Eighteen

Leah felt a cold hollow open in her chest and immediately put the phone on the kitchen counter. It was like he'd touched her again. Her eyes didn't shift from the words on the screen. How had he got her number? When she'd passed out, had he gone through her contacts?

Upstairs a floorboard creaked as Elliot moved about his room.

She reread the message several times. She had to tell Elliot. Turning around she stepped uncertainly to the doorway. Ahead of her were the stairs and the spot at the base of them she should walk to and call him down.

But she closed the door, as if he'd be able to hear the turmoil in her head.

Think. Think for a few seconds.

She took a faltering half breath, read the message again. What would be Elliot's reaction? She'd kissed a man she'd only known for minutes. A murderer. She wiped her palms against each other. But if she told Elliot, she'd then have to tell the police. He'd insist on that. She'd withheld from them. But only because she felt so foolish.

She'd been in shock. He'd offered her comfort in what she'd assumed, what anyone would have assumed, had been his home.

Elliot's feet thudded overhead, and a drawer slid open.

Leah had wanted to stay in his embrace though. That was what repelled her now. She'd wanted to linger there. And she'd gone back to the house because of that.

But only she knew that.

You've done nothing wrong. He kissed you. You made excuses and left soon after. But she'd already concealed it.

Why should she care how Elliot reacted? He'd barely asked her about the incident when he'd come in drunk. She'd been angry because Elliot hadn't been there to help her. He'd been out on Valentine's night with God knows who. Maybe he was going back to stay with them now.

She had to tell the police. No question. But she would deal directly with DI Byrne. There was no need for Elliot to be involved. She'd told Martin Tate where she lived but that didn't mean he'd want to find her there. He could have done anything to her that night. When she was unconscious. Why hadn't he?

It was probably Elliot that had left the door on the latch. Let him head off to wherever he intended to go and she could sort it out directly with the police. With any luck they'd apprehend Martin Tate, or whatever his real name was, and, bar her statement, her involvement would be over.

But Leah didn't believe her own reassurance for a

second. She was a witness. Would she have to recount her experience in court? With Martin Tate standing in front of her? With Elliot there? Leah felt nausea rise. He'd carried her into the lounge, given her alcohol, she'd accepted, and he'd kissed her before she went back the following morning with a gift ... a gift for Alice Booth's killer.

It felt like there was a stampede in her chest.

Had he really gone through her phone when she was oblivious? Wait though, she'd used his landline. Had he just redialled the last number? That was Elliot's phone she'd called though. He had to have got her number from her contacts. But he couldn't have accessed those without her fingerprint.

An image of her lying on the kitchen floor with him crouching over her and pushing her finger against the sensor button on her phone popped into her head.

For the first time all of her rationalising about how the whole situation was somehow a misunderstanding, and that Martin Tate could be as much an innocent as she was, slid away. Had he killed Alice Booth before she'd knocked on his door? Or had she been tied up upstairs, still alive, all the time he'd been so helpful to Leah?

Her forehead stung cold. She looked through the locked French doors into the garden. Where had he sent this message from? Somewhere nearby? And why? Because he believed nobody had found Alice Booth's body yet? The police had said she was meant to be going on holiday.

'I've barely got enough clothes for the weekend.'

Leah jumped and spun around to find Elliot standing in the kitchen doorway with a sports bag in his hand. She'd been so caught up in her thoughts she hadn't heard him come down the stairs and push the door.

'Sorry.' His expression shifted to concern when he saw hers. 'Are you OK? You look really white.'

'Just … feeling jittery.'

'I'm not surprised. I don't think we should come back here until they've caught this guy.' He went to the tumble drier, dumped down the bag and started pulling out some clothes.

'You should go as soon as you've got what you need.'

Elliot paused, hand inside the machine, and frowned. 'I'm not leaving here until you do.'

Leah had made up her mind. She would get Elliot out of the way and then talk to the police on her own. 'I've just had a call. They want me to walk over and pick the car up.'

Elliot's frown deepened. 'I thought they were dropping it back.'

Leah picked up her phone as if it could betray her. 'They've not got anyone available. I don't mind walking over. I can drive straight on to Dad's from there.'

Elliot stood and put his hands on his hips. 'They expect you to go back over there? After what happened?'

'Maybe they want to ask me some more questions.'

He threw a shirt into his bag. 'I'll come with you.'

'No,' she said too abruptly.

He seemed hurt by the reaction.

'You really don't have to. You're the one who said we need to be living more independently now.' But Leah didn't believe that.

'Forget it. I need to know you're going to be OK.'

If it had been a conversation at another time, Leah would have been glad to hear the words. But now he was just making things difficult. 'Please, Elliot. The sooner we're both away from here the better. How are you getting to … where you're going?' she deflected.

'I can … hop on the train,' he replied awkwardly. 'But that can wait. I really think I should go with you.'

Why did it sound like he might *not* be getting the train? Leah didn't have time to speculate. And she didn't want to tell him any more lies. 'I'll be fine. Go and catch your train. I'll grab a few things and then I'll be off too.'

'I've told you; I'm not leaving here until you do.'

'OK.' Leah gripped her phone tight as she passed him. 'I'll just need a couple of minutes.'

'You're sure you're all right?'

When Leah turned she could see he hadn't been convinced by her performance.

'If you want me to, I can come with you to your dad's.'

She could tell the offer was genuine. But at that moment the phone buzzed in her hand again.

Chapter Nineteen

Leah hoped it wasn't Fitch calling her and strode quickly through the hallway to the stairs. It only buzzed once, however, so it had to be a message. Her shoulders stiffened as she climbed.

'Leah?' Elliot was standing in the hallway looking up at her.

'Just give me a minute.' Cold flushed through her as she walked into the bedroom, closed the door and sat on the end of the bed. Girding herself, she opened the message.

What are your plans this weekend? Feel bad that Elliot made you miss out on Valentine's Day.

Leah pressed her feet hard to the floor. It was another reference to a conversation they'd had. How did he know Elliot's name? She must have used it when she called him from Alice Booth's landline. But she couldn't remember doing that. Even if she didn't allow Elliot to see this, she had to show the messages to the police.

If he was asking her about her plans for the day did that mean he was still in the area? He knew where she was. Leah walked to the window and looked out. It overlooked the front drive and the road in front of the house. Two cars went by in quick succession but there was nobody else in sight.

Was it even safe to go out there? But it was daytime. Surely nothing could happen to her on a busy Saturday morning. But then she considered how she'd assumed everything was normal inside Alice Booth's house, when looking in one of the other rooms would have told her otherwise.

Why did he want to meet her? To dispose of her? But she reminded herself he'd had ample opportunity to do that the night before. Whatever his motive—

The phone buzzed again.

Elliot at home? Understand if it's awkward.

Her breath locked in her chest. She read the three messages that had arrived. It now looked like she'd exchanged much more information with a murderer than she'd led the police to believe. She had to stop it. How many more intimate details would he use?

Give yourself in to the police.

She typed quickly but her finger paused over 'send'.

This was a mistake. She knew it was. She shouldn't engage with him. But she had to stop his texts. What would his next message insinuate?

'How long does it take to pack a bag?' Elliot shouted up the stairs.

Leah wondered how long she'd been. It felt like seconds but as she checked the time of his second message arriving, she saw it had been seven minutes ago.

There was tumping on the stairs.

Elliot was on his way up. She had to make a decision before another text arrived.

Leah hit 'send'. It was done. Now Alice Booth's murderer would know he could no longer dupe her.

The door half opened and then paused. Elliot knocked. Two years ago, he would have just walked in. Leah used the gap to open the wardrobe and slide out her overnight bag. She managed to dump it on the bed before he put his head in.

'Nearly ready?' He regarded the empty holdall.

'Just give me two minutes.'

His eyes remained on the bag. 'We really shouldn't hang around.'

She nodded emphatically. 'Lock up and I'll be down by the time you've done it.'

'OK,' he said uncertainly before his gaze slid to the phone in her hand.

'Just texting Dad.'

'OK,' he repeated, warily. 'I won't take long.'

'Nor will I.' She opened the top drawer of the dresser and grabbed a handful of underwear.

Elliot stomped back downstairs and Leah took a breath. She looked at her phone display, dreading another message appearing. That had to have scared him off. But when she told the police she'd have to explain why she'd let their prime suspect know they were onto him. Did he believe he'd have the time Alice Booth was meant to be on holiday before she was missed?

Leah knew she had to focus. She threw the underwear, a few tops, a few pairs of trousers and her toilet bag into her overnight and headed downstairs.

Elliot was waiting in the hallway with his light-blue hooded jacket on.

'Everything secure?'

'Yes,' he sighed.

Leah realised she'd probably taken longer than she'd said.

'Are you really OK?'

Leah dumped her bag down so she didn't have to meet his eye. 'As OK as can be expected.'

'There's nothing else you're not telling me.' He waited for her to straighten.

'What wouldn't I be telling you?'

He looked past her eyes with his deep brown gaze.

'What time is your train?'

He knew she was changing the subject but looked uncomfortable. 'I don't know.'

'Let's just...' She nodded at the front door and hefted her bag.

Elliot said nothing as he opened it.

Leah carried her bag to the end of the drive and hoped

Fitch wasn't about to turn up with the car. There was no sign of it approaching when she stepped into the street.

They both anxiously scanned their surroundings.

'I'm off this way.' Elliot slung his bag over his shoulder. 'You're sure you don't want me to come with you?'

Leah did. But then Leah still had to deceive him again. 'I'll call you when I get to Dad's.'

He nodded.

Leah turned first. 'Speak to you in a couple of hours.' She headed down the street. She could stop off in Langtry's and call Fitch. She would ask to speak to DI Byrne. Better that than have the same conversation twice. Maybe it would be easier speaking to a woman but she doubted the female detective would understand why she'd omitted such a significant part of her account. She walked briskly, her eyes darting about as she dreaded glimpsing a familiar, tanned face.

Chapter Twenty

L eah tried to acknowledge the small talk of Andre, the owner of Langtry's, and found herself a stool in the window of the café but sat there for only a few moments before she walked out. Andre called out a puzzled goodbye to her and she turned and waved before heading towards the high street.

She hadn't called Fitch because now she was unsettled by Elliot's behaviour. Was he really getting on a train? It hadn't sounded like he was. What was he up to? Or was Leah just using it as an excuse not to have the conversation she needed to with the police? But she had to make sure he really was leaving and wanted him as far away from the house as possible. She halted and glanced at her watch. Local trains were ten to the hour and it was only just gone half past nine. Heading back up Minster Street she decided to quickly check the little station. Make sure he got on a train. Then she would walk to Plough Lane via the bowling green, have the conversation with DI Byrne, pick up Elliot's car and drive to her dad's.

Leah checked the cars on both sides of the road. All empty. No watchful occupants. And the faces of the pedestrians she scrutinised bore no resemblance to the man she'd met the night before. A young family she recognised passed her and she remembered to smile and say hi. Everything seemed so ordinary.

When she reached the house she marched quickly by. Even though Fitch and Elliot had checked all the rooms she was still unnerved by the presence of the duck in the kitchen. Where had Martin Tate been when he'd sent her the messages?

'Hi, Rhian.'

Mr Trent, her grey-bearded neighbour, had appeared at the end of his drive. He always got her name wrong. Mr Trent was probably mid-sixties and had lived next door ever since she and Elliot had moved in. Mrs Trent was always baking for them and making gentle enquiries about them having a family. Neither of them was aware of her and Elliot's current circumstances.

Mr Trent grabbed his black recycling bin and started pulling it noisily up his driveway but then paused. 'Was that Elliot I saw going off earlier?'

Leah was in no mood for small talk but Mr Trent was always a sweetheart to her and she didn't want to be rude to him. 'Yes. Away on his own today.'

Mr Trent nodded and then pulled a pained expression that accentuated the wrinkles on his bald head. 'Are *you* OK?'

Leah frowned. 'I'm fine.'

'Elliot too?'

'Uh … yes.' Where was he going with this?

'If you ever need to talk, you know where Trudy is.'

'Thanks… That's good to know…' She had to ask. 'Why the offer?'

Mr Trent glanced briefly over his shoulder. 'I told Trudy to stay out of things, but she just wants you to know she's here if you need an ear.'

Leah put down her overnight bag. 'What would I need to talk to Trudy about?'

Mr Trent immediately held up his hand. 'None of my business. And none of Trudy's either. I won't get a minute's peace if I don't let you know though. So there, I've passed it on so now you can tell us both to keep our noses out.'

'I really don't know what you're talking about.' Was it so obvious to people that she and Elliot were having problems?

'We'd just hate to see you both throw away what you have.' It was Trudy Trent. She was walking down the driveway in a blue apron, wiping her hands on the front of it. Her grey hair was drawn back into a tight bun on the top of her head and she moved her squat and considerable frame surprisingly nimbly to join them.

How long should she keep the mystified frown going? 'We're fine, thanks,' Leah lied. This was definitely a conversation she didn't want to have now.

'Told you.' Mr Trent sighed at his wife.

'You must think we're interfering…' But there was genuine concern on Mrs Trent's face.

Leah let her flail for words. Were she and Elliot the regular subject of discussion in the Trents's home?

'...with all of the comings and goings, though, it's difficult not to notice.'

'What comings and goings?'

'Leave it now, Trudy,' Mr Trent warned his wife. His face was turning crimson with embarrassment.

Mrs Trent seemed to consider that.

'What comings and goings?' Leah repeated.

'I saw Elliot with that young woman last night,' Mrs Trent said quickly, as if she wasn't sure whether Leah was hearing about it for the first time or not.

Woman? Leah felt a spike of dismay but shrugged, like she knew exactly what Mrs Trent was talking about. 'When he got home?' she asked, as if she was about to confirm a misunderstanding.

'Yes.' Mrs Trent gestured at her husband. 'He was just closing the blinds in our bedroom.'

Mr Trent shook his head. 'I wasn't spying.'

'I know who dropped him off.' At least, Elliot had told her that a scooter man had dropped him off in the car.

It was Mrs Trent's turn to frown. 'So you know her?'

Leah nodded, kept her lips shut tight.

'Sorry, I didn't want to land Elliot in trouble. It really isn't our business.'

Mr Trent rolled his eyes at his wife.

'You're both ... involved with other people now?'

Leah considered how to answer her. So a woman had given Elliot a ride home in his own car. 'We're living together but apart ... for the time being.'

The disappointment registered in both the Trents's eyes.

'So ... if you were a little surprised by Elliot's behaviour...' Leah hoped Trudy would elaborate.

'I closed the blind. Took me by surprise, that's all.' Mr Trent shot a scathing look at his wife. 'Trudy opened it again.'

'Only because I didn't believe what he'd told me,' Mrs Trent replied weakly.

'What was it that surprised you so much?' Leah tried to sound matter-of-fact but wanted to know the answer as much as she didn't.

'Them kissing.' Mrs Trent looked uncomfortable. 'He was still kissing her when I came to the window.' Her eyes were on the tarmac. 'And how angry she seemed with him when she walked off down the street.'

Chapter Twenty-One

Leah struggled to compose her emotions. Even though she'd told herself that it was very likely, actually knowing for sure that Elliot was involved with another woman still winded her. It also sounded like whoever she was lived nearby. Why else would she have walked away from their house? She'd always assumed that, if Elliot was seeing someone else, it would be a girl he'd met at work or in a social situation related to it. Was she right on Leah's doorstep? They knew a lot of people by name in their small village, but all of their real friends lived outside Forley. There was nobody nearby with whom they spent any significant time.

'Maybe we've said too much.' Mr Trent reacted to her expression.

'You're not telling me anything I don't know,' Leah said dismissively. But having her suspicions confirmed by the neighbours was the last thing she'd expected.

'Are you sure you're OK?' Mrs Trent clearly didn't believe Leah's assurance.

She nodded. But a hundred questions were already whizzing around her head. Was it someone from the coffee shop or a woman he met up with when he went for his local runs? Or was that a deceit, an excuse to visit somebody who only lived a few streets away?

'Come on in, Trudy.' Mr Trent rolled the recycle bin a few feet up the drive but stopped when his wife didn't follow.

'I'm sorry. We assumed because of your own situation...' Mrs Trent began to explain.

'What did you assume?' Leah couldn't keep the harshness from her voice.

'We're sad to see things going wrong for both of you, that's all.'

'And what do you mean, because of my own situation?'

'Leave it now, Trudy!' Mr Trent barked.

But she didn't acknowledge her husband. 'Whatever you think of me, Leah, I don't make a habit of prying into your business but sometimes we see things we don't intend to.'

The clamour in Leah's brain briefly halted. 'Sorry, what are you talking about now?'

'The man who came to call here.'

Leah shook her head at Mrs Trent. 'I honestly don't know what you're talking about.'

'Trudy!' Mr Trent held up his hand. 'Sorry, my wife's overstepped the mark.'

'It's OK.' Leah was more intrigued than angry. 'I'd like to know who this male caller is.'

'He's right. I really don't want to fall out with you, Leah.'

'You can't leave it there.' What had Mrs Trent seen? But Leah was hard pushed to remember another man that had been in the house in the last few months.

Mrs Trent swivelled to follow her husband up the driveway.

'Mrs Trent, I'd honestly love to know. I'm sure you've got the wrong idea though.'

Mrs Trent halted and turned. 'You're right. I probably have.'

But Leah could tell her neighbour was just trying to placate her.

'Please, if you saw a man here there'll be a legitimate reason.'

'Even if he let himself out at night when you were home and Elliot wasn't?' Mrs Trent raised both eyebrows.

'Trudy, that's enough!'

But Mrs Trent's expression remained suspended, daring Leah to deny it.

Leah was momentarily stunned. 'When was this?'

Mrs Trent headed up the driveway.

Leah racked her brains. There had to be an occasion she could relate to what she'd just been told. But she couldn't think of anything. 'Mrs Trent...'

Mrs Trent didn't look back.

Leah marched up the drive until she caught up with them both. 'Wait.'

They turned and Mrs Trent regarded her coolly.

'I don't know what you saw but it wasn't what you thought.'

Mrs Trent nodded, as if humouring her.

'A man letting himself out of the house at night? Are you sure it wasn't Elliot?'

'I'm positive it wasn't.'

Leah's eyes shot briefly to Mr Trent but his face was impassive. 'You saw this?'

He nodded and looked down at his shoes.

'And why were you *so* sure it wasn't Elliot?'

'Because he came home in a car immediately after.' Mrs Trent didn't blink.

Leah was speechless.

'Watched him get out of the car with that girl. Give her that long kiss good night before she strutted away.'

Leah tried to process what she'd just been told. 'So you saw this man leaving my house last night?'

Mrs Trent nodded, her face sceptical. 'That's why I'm sure you should remember.'

Chapter Twenty-Two

Ten hours earlier

Tate stood in the garden and watched the bathroom window for a further couple of minutes, anticipating her emergence from the shower and the movement of her body in front of the frosted window as she dried herself. He wasn't a pervert. He should look away now. He told himself that as soon as he saw a sign of her, he would. But the hiss of the water continued. Was she OK up there?

Another minute passed. There hadn't been any other activity. Elliot clearly wasn't home. He peered down the narrow, dark gap on the right side of the house, between the wall and next door's fence. More weak light spilled out about halfway along.

Keeping his eyes fixed on the bathroom window Tate moved back towards the kitchen and then turned his body sideways so he could slide through the gap. He came to a small window and looked in. It was the downstairs lavatory and the door was open into the kitchen. He could see the breakfast bar with two tall stools under it. There was a metal basket of red and green peppers on top. No sign of anyone else.

He remembered the garage at the front and continued along the wall until he was standing at the top of the driveway, his back to its closed door. He cast his eyes along the windows of the houses opposite, but most were in darkness or had curtains drawn. He kept facing them, bent his legs and slid his hands behind him and under the metallic edge of the door. He took the weight in his knees and arms and lifted. The door squeaked as it started to rise. His body tensed and he halted. Then he raised it slowly, reducing the sound, until the door was high enough for him to slip inside.

The strip bulbs were bright in there but there was no car parked. It smelt of oil and wood shavings. He made his way to the door to the right and paused to listen. No sound from the other side. The light on told him she'd been in the garage since she'd got back. Checking Elliot was home? He put his fingers around the handle and wasn't surprised when he depressed it and the door clicked open.

He was looking into the kitchen, seeing the red and green peppers from a different angle. Nobody else around. He stepped into it from the garage and carefully closed the door behind him.

The room was cold but he could hear the boiler running. Sounded like Leah Talbot was still in the shower. He walked stealthily into the carpeted hallway and paused at the open lounge door. The light was on in there too. Looked like a little home office had been set up in the window. He took in the sparse furnishings. Was this where she spent her days? Or maybe this was hubby's lair. He spotted an array of framed photos on the dresser and crossed the room to examine them.

She was with him in three of them. One of them was a wedding photograph. Looked like quite a scaled-back event at a small church. Elliot grinned back, clenching his teeth to prove how happy he was. He picked up the photo of their two black and white faces. It looked like the most recent one. Elliot was fuller in the face and didn't clench as hard in this one. His eyes looked distracted by something beyond the lens.

He replaced the photo in its exact position and felt an irrational sense of hostility towards Elliot. Anger was an emotion that rarely troubled him. Everything he did was deliberate, premeditated and clinical. Being in this house now was none of those things. It was time to leave, but first he wanted to make sure she was OK.

The boiler continued to run.

He stole to the bottom of the stairs and hesitated. The noise of the water trickled down from upstairs, odd flurries indicating the movement of her body. So she was fine. Go.

But Tate surveyed the stairs that were carpeted in the same deep blue as the hallway. He started to climb them, stepping on the edges nearest the wall to avoid creaks giving away his presence.

He couldn't prevent a few squeaks and paused every time, waiting for the shower to be switched off. But it didn't and it was still hissing when he reached the top. A thin ribbon of light cut across the blue carpet of the landing and as he crossed to the door emitting it a floorboard groaned. He held his breath, waited for a reaction. But the water kept flowing. Her ears would be full of it. He could probably speak to her from where he was standing, and she wouldn't hear.

He was comfortable trespassing in the homes of strangers. Knew exactly how little was required to remain hidden and how to sidestep into the spaces outside everyday circuits. But he hadn't studied Leah yet and he couldn't put himself at risk.

The door was ajar about half an inch and he placed the tip of his forefinger on the stained panel and gave it a gentle nudge. He looked beyond the edge as it opened slightly inwards and through the steamed atmosphere. The washing basket was open, her familiar clothes dumped inside.

Leah was sitting in the cubicle, side on to him, her back against the champagne tiles as the water trickled over her. Her eyes were closed.

An aroma drifted out at him, carried by the vapour. An artificial fruit detergent scent with a human smell underscoring it.

He could see the side of her face, her throat, her shoulder, her breast, her nipple, her thigh, her calf, her foot. One still half of a whole. The skin binding her together was pale. There was a red bra-strap mark on the top of her shoulder. Then she drew in breath and it moved everything. She opened her mouth to exhale and released a sigh.

Water tumbled from her and her foot squeaked as she started to move. To stand.

The tableau had kept him in the doorway longer than he wanted to allow himself and a vague internal alarm suddenly became louder. He took his fingertip away from the door and it swung back to its original position, blocking his view of her.

Any moment, she would be turning the dial, halting the flow and removing his cover. He had to go now if he wanted his exit down the stairs to go unnoticed. But he stayed where he was, the warm moisture cold on his chin in the draught of the landing. What if he remained where he was? Let her find him there when she opened the door?

He tried to imagine her reaction. How the muscles in her face would reconfigure themselves. Fright first, then realisation, recognition and then terror. And beyond that? Would Leah Talbot remember what had passed briefly between them earlier and understand why he'd followed her there?

He put his fingertip on the door again. Considered how exerting slightly more force than he had the first time would reveal him and trigger an alternative event to the one his survival instincts told him was necessary.

The water kept running.

He tensed his finger, tempted by the notion of breaking the barrier between them. He could hear her feet moving about in the cubicle.

But a moment later he was treading carefully back down the stairs, retracing the path he'd negotiated up them in reverse. He stopped at the bottom and looked up, the moisture still cooling on his chin.

The water stopped. The boiler downstairs cut out a few seconds after.

He could hear the last liquid running down the plughole. She'd be getting out soon. Pulling on a robe. She couldn't know he'd been there. He decided to slip out through the front door. It was the quickest way to exit the house. He painstakingly turned the handle.

Tate walked out into the cold rain but barely noticed it, delicately clicked the door closed behind him and strode down the drive.

He had to leave now because tomorrow he intended to come back.

Chapter Twenty-Three

'What did he look like?' Leah dreaded the Trents's answer.

'I know it wasn't Elliot,' Mr Trent said apologetically.

'I understand that. Describe him though.'

'Difficult to say. It was really dark.' He shifted uncomfortably.

'This is really important. Anything at all. What was his hair like?'

'Fair hair.' He seemed positive of that.

The tops of Leah's shoulders bristled.

'Slim build. Average height. That's all I can really remember.'

'What was he wearing?'

'I don't recall.' Mr Trent exchanged a worried look with his wife.

'Are you sure?'

Mr Trent nodded.

'And what did he do after he came out of my house?'

'Just walked out of the drive and turned into the street.'

'Which way?'

'Right, I think.' He took in her reaction. 'Right, I'm sure.'

'You didn't see where he went? Or if he got into a car?'

'No.'

Mrs Trent's hostility had evaporated. 'What's this all about? Are you saying you didn't know him?'

Leah turned when she heard the car. She recognised Fitch's brown Audi as it slowed outside her home. 'Do you both mind waiting here?' she said as it pulled in and parked. 'This is the police.'

'Police?' Mrs Trent's face lit up.

Leah registered that Fitch hadn't brought her car back. 'Just a minute. Don't go anywhere.'

Leah trotted down the drive. 'There's been a development.'

Fitch was just heading into her house and turned in surprise as she emerged from next door. 'Yes, there has. Would you mind coming with me?'

'I mean, I had something to tell you. Somebody was in my home last night and it sounds like Martin Tate.'

Fitch's expression froze.

'My neighbours have just told me. Ask them.' She indicated the couple watching their exchange.

Fitch said nothing but moved past her and approached the Trents.

Leah followed and waited as the officer introduced himself. 'Tell him what you just told me.'

They did and Fitch nodded before repeating the questions she'd just asked them.

'How was he acting? Was there anything furtive about his behaviour?'

Mr Trent glanced briefly at Leah. 'I wouldn't say that.'

'He was relaxed then, not particularly conscious of being spotted?'

'I suppose so.'

Leah watched Fitch purse his lips. What did it look like to the three of them? That she'd invited him back and that her guest had left casually afterwards?

'And what time was this?'

'Trudy and I went to bed between half twelve and one so it would have been around then.'

'After I got home but just before Elliot did. I had a shower and then found my husband downstairs.'

'And you didn't hear any sounds in the house?'

'No. I would have mentioned them to you before now if I had.' Leah tried to keep the exasperation out of her voice.

'You didn't hear the front door opening or closing?'

'No, again, I would have mentioned that.'

'And nor did your husband?'

Leah took a short inward breath. 'I said, he wasn't home at that point. I heard the front door when Elliot got in.'

'But we both saw Elliot when he did come home.' Mrs Trent was clearly feeling left out of the conversation.

Leah nodded at Mrs Trent. 'It's OK to tell him. I've got nothing to hide.'

'He was dropped off by a young lady. She was driving and got out to talk to him and kiss him before she walked off down the road.'

Fitch met Leah's eye. 'Do you know this woman?'

Leah shook her head once and ignored Mrs Trent's reaction.

'And when was that?'

'Like I said, Elliot came in just after I'd had my shower. So about half an hour after I got in.'

'You don't have any security cameras on the property?'

Mr Trent shook his head.

Leah already knew that. Had the man who claimed to be Martin Tate followed her home and got inside her house while she'd been washing the smell of the deer off in the shower? Her stomach shrivelled.

Fitch turned to her. 'There were no signs of a break-in?'

'You saw yourself when you took a look around earlier.'

'Aside from the front door being on the latch,' Fitch reminded her.

'Elliot could have done that this morning though.'

Fitch turned things over in his head. 'Where's Elliot now?'

'Um ... he went off to the station.' She checked her watch. It was five to ten. His train would have left by now. *If* he'd been telling the truth about getting on it. Leah knew the next question was inevitable.

'Where's he gone?'

Leah took in three expectant expressions. 'I don't know.'

Chapter Twenty-Four

'So, why can't I have my car returned?' Leah was sitting in Fitch's passenger seat as he drove them back through Forley.

'You can. DI Byrne needs a word with you first though.'

'About what? I just want to get away from here now. My dad's expecting me. He has Alzheimer's and no day carer this afternoon.'

Fitch nodded, understanding. 'If that was the same man in your house last night...'

'*If*? It couldn't have been anyone else.' She had to tell DI Byrne about the messages she'd received.

'If it was, he may not be a danger to you now. He called Alice Booth's home phone.'

Leah took a moment to absorb what he'd said. 'When?'

'About fifteen minutes ago. Called the landline. Unlikely to be a crank so soon after the event. Plus he knew the details of the scene too intimately.'

'You spoke to him?'

'No. DI Byrne did. Said he wants to give himself up.'

Leah felt a surge of relief but it was short-lived. Surely that couldn't be anything to do with the message she'd sent back to him. She'd have to admit to that now. '"Give himself up"?'

Fitch nodded.

'When?'

'Says he'll phone with a location for later today.'

'Why not straightaway?'

'That's what DI Byrne asked him. Claims he's got a few loose ends to tie up.'

Leah needed to open the window. 'D'you think I'm one of them?'

'That's why she sent me to pick you up. There's an unmarked car getting into position to watch your house. Just for safety. You're sure your husband won't return home?'

'I'll call him and double check.' Leah shakily took out her phone.

'DI Byrne was only doing it as a precaution but after your neighbours' story...'

Elliot's number rang but she got his answering service. 'It's me. Please call me as soon as you get this. Let me know you're OK.' *Whoever you're with.* 'And don't go home, under any circumstances. It looks like somebody did break in last night so the police are concerned he might come back. I'll explain everything else when I speak to you.' She hung up.

'You think he'll get that message?'

128

'Eventually. I'm sure he's on a train though.' But she wasn't.

Fitch caught the worry in her expression. 'If he does call at the house, there'll be officers in attendance.'

Leah wondered if Elliot was still in Forley with the woman who had driven him home last night. She still hadn't begun to deal with that revelation. 'Do you believe Tate?'

'It's rare for somebody to give themselves up so soon after a crime was committed but it's been known.'

'D'you think it's because I'm a witness?'

'Perhaps. You do realise that didn't have to be the case though.'

Leah knew exactly what he meant. Tate didn't have to let her go. 'Maybe there's another explanation.' Leah so wanted that to be the truth. 'Of why he was there and why what happened … happened.'

Fitch sucked in air through his teeth. 'He's certainly got a lot of explaining to do.' He turned right at the roundabout that took them back to Plough Lane.

Leah wanted to ask exactly how Alice Booth had died. It was a question she'd put at the back of her mind since she'd first learnt of her murder. But she was sure Fitch wouldn't divulge those details. Maybe his boss would. Leah had to know, even though she didn't want to.

The Audi slowed at the traffic lights. A right turn and they would be back at the house. But Leah had changed her mind. If Martin Tate handed himself in then his messages to her wouldn't be as relevant. She'd told the police that he'd followed her home and had broken in and she was still trying to repel the notion of him being inside her house while she'd been in the shower. But if she could spare herself the ordeal of relaying the contents of the messages...

She couldn't plead ignorance of them arriving. She'd opened them and there would be a record of that. But if Martin Tate surrendered she hoped his deceiving her would be secondary to the crime he'd committed against Alice Booth.

If he didn't, she had no choice but to give up the texts. Was she just forestalling the inevitable? But maybe there was a larger part of Martin Tate's story that nobody understood, that he needed to convey to the police as soon as possible.

She was positive that she wasn't about to disentangle herself from what had happened, however. If he was lying about his willingness to cooperate, did that make her a prime suspect? Was she already?

Fitch pulled up in front of the house. Elliot's car was still parked in the same position. Had they fingerprinted it?

DI Byrne was just walking out of the gates, talking on her phone.

With rising dread, Leah got out of the car and took her overnight bag from the back seat.

'All right, on my way there now.' Byrne hung up.

Fitch quickly filled her in on the Trents spotting the familiar figure leaving Leah's house the night before.

Byrne didn't look at Leah but tried unsuccessfully to hide her surprise. 'You've left a car there?'

'Lloyd.'

'Send a second car. Make sure they stay out of sight.'

Fitch relayed the instructions to another officer.

Byrne turned to Leah. 'You know about our caller?'

'Yes.'

'You're my only witness. If he does give himself up, I want you to be present.'

Chapter Twenty-Five

'Y ou want me to confirm it's him?'

DI Byrne, seeing Leah's panicked expression, held up a placatory hand. 'We'll find a place to conceal you.'

Leah felt a sudden rush of anxiety.

'We'll go in my car.' Byrne nodded at a white Lexus.

She focused on Elliot's blue Vauxhall. 'Can't I go in mine? I don't really want to leave it parked on such a busy road.'

'It'll be fine. Jump in.' Byrne opened her car with the fob.

The locks thudded but Leah was still examining her vehicle. Had they been inside it? She could still see the bottle of red wine on the dash.

'It'll be perfectly safe. There'll be officers here for the foreseeable. I need to give forensics their space, so we'll head back now.'

Leah felt in a daze. 'Aren't you waiting for his call?'

'Somebody's manning the phone until we get the

number transferred.' Byrne extended her arm, indicating that Leah should walk ahead to the car.

She complied, got into the passenger seat of the Lexus and slid her overnight bag into the back. The interior smelt overpoweringly of coffee. There was a half-full paper cup in the holder.

'Seat belt,' Byrne said before she closed her door too.

Leah obeyed. It was good advice as Byrne pulled jerkily out of the spot and headed back down Plough Lane.

'You must be feeling pretty shaken.' Byrne tugged her belt on as they slowed at the bend.

'I don't ever want to go home now.' Leah wasn't exaggerating.

'Understandable. Where's your husband?'

Everyone wanted to know that, and she still wasn't sure. 'Gone to stay with a friend.'

Byrne nodded. 'You going to stay with them too?'

'I'm going to visit my father,' Leah said, deflecting the question.

'Where does he live?'

'Brockford.'

'Nearby then,' Byrne observed.

'Less than twenty miles from here. He's got Alzheimer's, which he's managing at the moment, but I'm glad he's close,' she heard herself answer. Did the police not want her travelling far?

Byrne nodded. 'When we're finished, would you mind leaving the address with me?'

So that answered that question.

'So neither you nor your husband were aware that the suspect got into the house?'

Leah shook her head. 'Only our neighbours saw it. There was no sign of a break-in when your colleague took a look around.'

'He couldn't have got hold of a house key from you?' Byrne changed down a gear.

Leah hadn't considered that. Another terrifying possibility to consider.

'When you lost consciousness?'

Acid tingled in Leah's stomach. 'I used my key to let myself in.'

'Best you don't go back until we've got him.'

'D'you really think he's going to give himself up?'

'Stranger things have happened but ... no.'

'Why d'you think he called then?'

'Not sure yet. Maybe he needed to find out if we'd discovered the body.'

Leah wondered if that was because of the message she'd sent him. She flinched as she reluctantly recalled his lips on hers. 'Why bother to say he's going to give himself up?'

'Could be misdirection. Or perhaps he just gets a kick from giving us the runaround. I think he wouldn't take the risk of speaking to us unless there was a motive though.'

'Is it not possible that there's a whole side to what happened that we don't know about?'

Byrne turned and analysed Leah incredulously. 'You think he's innocent?'

'I didn't say that.'

'Whoever he is, he shouldn't have been at Alice Booth's house...'

'Do you know that for sure?'

Byrne shook her head. 'And nor should you have. But when you both left Alice Booth was dead.'

Leah opened her mouth to respond.

'And, after seventeen years in the job, I've never seen the sort of mutilation that she sustained.' Byrne met her eyes, a grimace briefly registering before she returned her attention to the road. Her phone buzzed.

'Yep?' The detective's eyes darted as she listened to the short message from the other end. 'Eleven?' The officer looked at her dash clock. 'OK. Get Fitch to co-ordinate some backup and I'll see you there.' She hung up. 'He called the house again,' she informed Leah. 'Wants to give himself up at the north gate of Eddington Park at eleven.' She put her foot on the accelerator.

Chapter Twenty-Six

F or the minutes that followed Leah remained silent as DI Byrne made calls and barked orders while she sped them towards the nearest large town. Eddington Park was just on the outskirts of Middleton.

'And tell Fitch I want somebody covering the east side.' Byrne hung up and slowed the car as they reached a roundabout.

'You're going to meet him?'

'Don't worry. You'll be in a separate car with another one of my officers. They're setting up there now. If he does show, you can ID him from your position.'

'But you don't think he's going to turn up?'

'If he genuinely wants to hand himself in, he could just walk into the police station. Why this song and dance?'

Leah had already asked herself that question. 'Perhaps he likes the attention.'

'No. I think he's exactly the opposite of that.' Byrne turned to her and, momentarily, it appeared she'd said all she wanted to. Then she added: 'This is no spur-of-the-moment homicide. This is a methodically executed crime. Wouldn't you say his behaviour towards you suggests that? He didn't have to open the front door to you, did he?'

Leah wondered if it was a rhetorical question. Did Byrne believe she was part of it, that him letting her in put suspicion on her? 'Do you really believe I could have anything to do with this?'

'Inviting you in, calling you a breakdown service from the crime scene ... that's not the behaviour of somebody who's just committed a murder on the premises, is it?'

But Leah acknowledged that she'd ignored her question.

'So until I can gauge the motives behind that I doubt very much that this meeting is going to be straightforward either.'

'But what if he's just going to watch us wait for him?'

'You'll be protected. And you'll be far enough away from the gates. We'll do as he says and just hope we can keep up the line of communication.'

'Why don't *you* think he attacked me in my house?'

Byrne gave an exaggerated shrug and raised her eyebrows, as if she were waiting for the answer from Leah.

'I was in the shower. I would have been defenceless.' She felt a jolt of horror as she considered how close he might have got.

Byrne nodded, encouraging her to continue.

'Why follow me home, break in and then do nothing?'

Byrne held up her hand. 'We're not positive he did nothing.'

'What else could he have done? I don't think he took

anything.' But that was difficult to know for sure. Or was Byrne insinuating something else?

'Your neighbours saw him leave. It was late. It was probably assumed he could do so unnoticed.'

Leah didn't like Byrne's choice of words. Did the detective think he'd been in the shower with her? 'Elliot was due home any moment.'

'Yes,' Byrne agreed flatly. 'He was. You'd phoned him about your accident.'

'Exactly.'

'Where had he been?'

Leah hated that she had no answer. 'He didn't tell me.'

'Not even when he got in?'

'No.'

'He's your husband. Don't you talk?'

'No, as a matter of fact.' Leah tried but failed to keep the anger out of her reply. 'The only reason we're not officially separated is because we're still living under the same roof. I have no idea where my husband was when I was stranded on the road in the dark. Maybe you should ask him and then maybe you can tell me.'

Byrne sniffed.

'I do know that he was with another woman though because she dropped him off in his own car and then kissed him goodnight. That fact I've just gleaned from my neighbours who saw it soon after a complete stranger walked out of my house.' Her temple pounded but she didn't regret raising her voice to Byrne.

'OK.' Byrne nodded slightly and they continued in silence until the police officer gestured ahead. 'This is us.'

Leah could see the green rusted railings of Eddington Park on their right. Byrne took a left turn then a right at the end. Halfway along the residential road a man in a tracksuit was standing on the right by some parked cars.

Byrne pulled them over and rolled down her window. 'Where's Travis?'

'Next right, then left. Ottway Crescent.'

Byrne didn't reply but pulled sharply away and followed his directions.

Leah clocked an older bald man with a grey moustache and a beer paunch, who she assumed was another plain-clothes officer. He stood up from the plastic seat of a bus stop and jogged over to the car.

'We can go a street further back if you want.'

Byrne cast her eyes around the other empty cars in the road. 'This'll be fine.'

'OK. There's a space further down on the right corner.' He pointed.

Byrne nodded and positioned the car where he'd indicated.

Leah looked right and could see the entrance to the park about fifty yards away on the other side of the busy street.

Byrne switched off the engine and glanced at her watch. 'Twenty minutes. How's your eyesight?'

Chapter Twenty-Seven

L eah remained in the Lexus while DI Byrne chatted to the other officer beside the car. She peered at the other vehicles around them and then the windows of the stucco houses that lined the street. There were so many places from which he could be watching them.

A young blonde girl in a bleached denim jacket emerged from a house a couple of doors down. She dropped the wheels of a pram onto the road and crossed it diagonally. Leah watched her as she passed and pushed her infant down towards the park gates.

Leah checked her phone. It was 10.43. Less than twenty minutes before he was due to appear. Where was Tate now? He had to know there'd be officers dotted around the location.

Byrne gestured for her to roll down her window. Leah did so and the officer bent down to speak to her.

'I'm going to make my way down there now.'

'You're meeting him alone?'

'No. But I don't want to spook him. Fitch will be just inside the entrance. He's making his way to it from the opposite side now.'

'D'you think Tate's in there?'

'He might not be coming that way. He may just walk up to it from the street, so we've got that covered as well. If he does decide to show, he won't get away.'

'But you still don't think he will?'

'We'll be prepared for every outcome,' Byrne said stolidly.

They both watched the young mother wheel her child to the crossing and pause to hit the button.

Byrne straightened. 'That's Travis.' She jerked her thumb at the other officer. 'He'll be right here with a radio. As soon as you recognise anyone, he'll let us know.'

Leah nodded. 'Are you going to be armed?'

'Fitch will have a taser. Just keep your eye on the gates and anyone in the near vicinity.'

Before Leah could utter another word, Byrne strode down the side street to join the mother at the crossing. She slid in a small earpiece as she walked.

Travis immediately opened the boot door hatch. 'You can see OK from there?'

Leah turned.

'Slide over to the driver's seat so you can get a better view. Just keep your eyes front and let me know if you spot him. I'll stay back here.'

'OK.' She obeyed and focused on the park gates. Two men in shorts with hipster beards jogged out and turned left.

The crossing beeps signalled the mother to cross and Byrne followed her to the other side.

Leah remembered to breathe and could taste the smog from the busy street on the back of her tongue.

Byrne slowed at the gates and then walked into the park.

Behind her Leah could hear Travis chewing gum and breathing through his nose.

Byrne looked left and right and then moved to one side as a male couple holding hands walked out of the gates. She lingered and then strolled out of the gates again and stood on the rampway.

Leah tried to keep track of the pedestrians hurrying by. It was a stretch to see at this distance, but she already felt they were too close. Could things really end this easily? Leah got the impression Byrne hadn't encountered anything like this before. Leah would be terrified in her position. What had Tate done to Alice Booth? She recalled the expression on Byrne's face when she'd stopped short of telling her. Was that because Leah never would have agreed to ID him?

A movement through the gates. Somebody walking down the main path towards them. It was still early. But he had to be nearby now. Leah narrowed her eyes at the man and recognised his face.

It was Fitch. He didn't acknowledge Byrne but seated himself on a bench about ten feet from the gates so he was in profile. That made Leah feel better. Now Byrne wasn't waiting there alone. If Tate were dangerous, was Fitch close enough to help her though?

The chewing behind her stopped. 'All in position.'

Leah realised he was talking softly into a radio.

Ten minutes passed but Leah's shoulders remained rigid. And Travis kept chewing. After a minute or so, Byrne walked a few paces left then a few right as Fitch pretended to be absorbed by the screen of his iPhone.

The traffic in and out of the park gradually increased. Leah blinked as she tried to keep up with the faces passing and crossing in front of Byrne.

'Just take a breath.' Travis clearly sensed her apprehension. 'We've still got three minutes before he's due.'

Leah nodded once. Squeezed her eyes briefly shut to moisturise them. There was a brief lull in the activity, but Byrne didn't once look in their direction.

'Who's this guy?'

Leah wasn't sure if Travis was talking directly to her or into his radio, but she could see who he was referring to. A man in a white baseball cap was walking from the right-hand side of the street and slowed as he reached the gates.

Was that him? With the hat on it was difficult to tell. He was wearing jeans and a tan casual jacket. She held her breath as he lingered there.

Byrne stepped back a pace as he hesitated outside, but he walked on past her and didn't enter the park.

'Could that have been him?'

Leah wasn't sure. 'Could have been.'

The man walked out of their field of vision. Byrne turned to watch him go.

'No positive ID. Let's see if he comes back.'

Leah rubbed her eyes. Perhaps he was going to come the way Fitch had. He still had his head bowed to his phone but was now perched right on the edge of the bench. He'd clearly thought that could have been their suspect too.

More pedestrians, more faces. Leah's eyes darted about them as the footfall increased.

'Just keep calm.' Travis started chewing again.

Leah's phone buzzed.

She opened it and looked at the message that had arrived. Her heart stumbled as she realised it was from her unknown caller.

Elliot says hi and not to tell police anything about our conversation.

Chapter Twenty-Eight

'E verything OK?' Travis asked from behind her. He'd clearly caught her intake of breath.

'Fine.' Leah held the phone against her leg so he couldn't see it. 'Just my husband. I need to call him back,' she heard herself lie.

Travis responded but Leah didn't hear him. Was this a bluff? Did Tate really expect her to believe that he had Elliot with him? She speed-dialled Elliot's number but as she held the phone tightly to her ear, she got his answering service.

'Any luck?'

'No,' she eventually replied, realising she'd got the beep and that her voice was now being recorded.

'If you can just concentrate on the park.'

The phone buzzed. Another message had arrived. A photo.

Leah surreptitiously opened it. It was of the back of Elliot as he walked down the street. He was wearing his hooded light-blue jacket and clutching his overnight bag. It had been taken that morning, as he'd headed off to the station. Leah's hand trembled as she took it in. Alice Booth's killer had been feet away as they'd both left the house.

'Can you contact him later?'

Leah nodded and turned her head right to look out of the window but her eyes were still on the image of her husband. Had Tate followed Elliot to the station? But what could he have done in broad daylight? Maybe he'd got on the train with him. Leah's mind raced. There was no denying the implication of the messages. Elliot's life was being threatened if she didn't stay silent. But how did Tate know she was with the police?

Leah's eyes darted around the street. Was he watching her right now?

'Anybody familiar yet?'

'Nobody.' Leah replied before returning her gaze to Byrne and Fitch at the park gates.

'OK, it's eleven, try to stay focused.'

But Leah suspected that nobody was about to arrive there and release her from the ordeal that had begun the moment she'd collided with the deer.

Byrne folded her arms and walked back a few paces to allow the human stream to pass, her eyes on each person that entered or exited the park.

Did Tate know Leah was here and was watching from a distance? He'd set up the whole meeting. He had to be. And, if that was the case, where was Elliot? Should she turn and tell Travis? Should she let him and Byrne know that they were wasting their time?

Somebody halted in front of Byrne.

Leah stiffened and peered hard, but the volume of traffic was obscuring them.

'Who's that?' Travis said aloud.

Leah craned forward.

Fitch stood up from the bench.

'Recognise them?'

'I can't see.' But it was clear they'd stopped to talk to Byrne.

'Is it him?' Travis demanded.

Leah shook her head. 'I still can't make them out properly.'

Fitch had already covered the space between the bench and the gates and was only a few feet away from Byrne.

Leah could see the back of the man as he spoke to the DI. He had a dark-blue hood pulled up.

Fitch reached Byrne and joined the confab.

'What's happening?' Travis walked into Leah's field of vision, radio to his mouth.

'I can't see his face.' Leah wanted to get out of the car.

'Unable to ID.' Travis spoke into his radio.

But why would he give himself up? Leah seized the opportunity to look around the street. No sign of him. But he could easily be concealed in a car or behind one of the windowpanes of the houses.

When Leah's eyes swung back to the park, Fitch was reversing his steps and Byrne was slightly shaking her head in their direction.

'It's a false alarm,' Travis confirmed.

The man in the hoodie tried to continue on his way but

Byrne took hold of his elbow. The man argued and she pulled out a badge.

Fitch returned to the group and put a restraining hand on the man's shoulder.

Travis took up his position at the rear of the car again.

Leah didn't turn to him. 'What's going on?'

'I think Byrne just got propositioned. Looks like she's going to hold him.'

Leah's thoughts skated between the messages she'd just received and the situation in front of her. She watched the two officers talking to the man and him gesticulating. He was much younger than Martin Tate. Probably only in his twenties. 'It's definitely not him.'

Fitch led the man to the bench and gestured for him to sit down. He refused and continued to argue.

Byrne's attention had returned to the pedestrians outside the park again.

The man was still complaining. Fitch took his arm and led him out of the park the other way.

'Where's he taking him?' Leah asked.

'Away from the situation. Don't want to frighten our boy away. Ignore that now. Just keep your eyes on the people around the gates.'

Leah tried to but didn't see Tate.

Half an hour later, Byrne returned to the car.

Chapter Twenty-Nine

'How much longer do I have to be here?' Leah rose from her plastic chair as soon as Fitch entered the poky interview room.

'Just a little longer,' he said appeasingly as he closed the door with his back.

There had been no further message from Martin Tate and Leah was getting increasingly uncomfortable being in the police station. She knew the longer she was there the more tempted she would be to tell them about the image that had been sent to her phone. Tate knew she was with the police and he'd warned her explicitly. She couldn't risk it. Couldn't risk losing Elliot. At least she was communicating with Tate and, so far, everything the DI knew about him had come from Leah. For whatever reason, Tate had singled her out and spared her life at Alice Booth's home and in her own. She had to use that. Tate had already proved he could effortlessly play the police and she'd already been at the station forty minutes while they interviewed the man who had propositioned Byrne outside the park.

'She'll be in to talk to you when she's finished. Can I get you a coffee?'

'No,' Leah replied a little abruptly. 'Are you actually holding me here?'

'You can go whenever you like...'

Leah knew there was a 'but' coming.

'But the DI wants to update you so you may as well wait here for now.'

'I need to sort out my dad's meal in half an hour.' That was true.

Sympathy registered on Fitch's face. 'She should be done soon. I'll let her know you need to get away.' He turned and opened the door.

As soon as it closed, she tried Elliot again for the umpteenth time. Leah hung up when she got his answering service. She opened the text messages and the one she'd sent back to the unknown number.

Have not spoken to police about messages. Please let me know Elliot is OK.

But she'd sent it on the drive to the station and there had been no response. Was he deliberately tormenting her? And if he had been at the park, had he followed her back here? Might he assume she was telling them everything and what did that mean for Elliot? She had to leave now. Fitch had said she could.

She lifted her handbag off the back of the chair but the

door opened.

DI Byrne entered and frowned.

'Just going to get myself a coffee.'

Fitch came in behind Byrne and met her eye suspiciously before he closed the door.

Leah reversed to the table.

Byrne folded her arms. 'I've just spoken to the man who approached me outside the park.'

Leah sat back down and waited for her to continue.

'Vincent Lownes. He was sticking with his story until I told him I was going to charge him with solicitation. Now he's admitted he was paid.'

'By who?'

'A man answering the description you gave us.'

So Tate *had* been there. Leah felt the desperate need to tell Byrne everything that was about to burst out of her.

'Lownes insists he's never seen the man before.'

'And you believe him?'

'He's professional homeless.' Byrne caught Leah's puzzlement. 'Has an address and a phone but sells *The Big Issue*. Looks like he has addiction issues. I've got a couple of officers scouring the east side of the park where the transaction took place, but our man will be long gone.'

'We're trying to access camera footage from the street opposite the east entrance but that's going to take time,' Fitch added.

'So, do you need me in the meantime?'

Byrne seemed slightly taken aback by Leah's impatience. 'Fitch said you're eager to visit your father...'

'I'm already late.'

Byrne unfolded her arms. 'You say he's in Brockford?'

Leah was slightly surprised but then recalled she'd told the officer during their journey to the park. 'Yes.'

Byrne took out her phone. 'Give me the address there.'

'3, Hock Cottage, Menthorn Drive.'

Byrne tapped her screen. 'I assume you'll have your mobile with you?'

Leah nodded. She'd already given them that number.

'OK.'

'I can go?' It seemed too good to be true.

'I'll be in touch with any news.'

'You don't need to interview me now?' *Shut up, Leah. Just get out of there.*

'We found one witness who saw you at the roadside last night. Your story checks out.' But Byrne seemed almost pained to admit it.

How long had the detective been sitting on that? She wasn't sure how to react.

'Just let us know if you plan to go further afield.'

Leah nodded and picked up her overnight bag. 'I will.'

She walked by her and Fitch opened the door. She was in a hurry. She'd told them that. But perhaps they were wondering why she seemed so unconcerned about Tate still being at large.

Was he waiting for her outside?

Chapter Thirty

'**D**o you need a ride?'

Leah turned only a few paces from the interview room.

Byrne was leaning out of the door. 'I brought you down here...'

In her rush to leave, Leah had forgotten that. 'No, that's fine, thank you. I'll call a cab.'

Byrne studied her uncertainly. 'Everything OK?'

'Fine. I just need to get to my father's.'

'Exactly why I'm offering.'

'You've got enough on your plate.'

'I won't be taking you, but I can certainly make someone available.'

'Thanks. No. You'll call me if there's any news?'

'I've just told you I will.'

'OK. We'll speak soon then.' Leah turned on her heel and strode down the corridor to the swing doors that led to reception. She had to get away from Byrne.

As soon as she'd walked out of the building she paused at the top of the steps and gulped cold, fresh air. She felt dizzy and steadied herself on the handrail.

'Are you all right?' A young uniformed officer was just ascending.

Leah nodded. 'I'll be fine.'

But he loitered there. 'Sure?'

'Yes. Fine,' she repeated pointedly.

'OK.' He moved by her.

Leah remained still until the wooziness passed then carried on down into the parking area.

A car screeched to a standstill then beeped at her as she crossed the concourse to the main entrance. She didn't meet the eye of the driver as she made her way out onto the busy street. Checking her phone she confirmed that there was still no further message from Tate. She sent another to him.

Please tell me what to do.

She waited but nothing came back. Was he watching her now? She cast her eyes around the pedestrians and parked cars but couldn't see a sign of him.

She kept moving away from Middleton Police Station and tried Elliot's number again. 'It's me. Please, please call me back the minute you get this,' she said to his answering service. Then Leah quickly made another call. It rang for a long time before it was picked up.

'Hello?' He sounded scared.

'Dad, it's Leah.'

There was a long pause. 'Hello, Leah,' he said, like he knew exactly who she was.

She was used to playing this game. She couldn't tell him directly that she was his daughter. That made him angry. More with himself than her. So she gave him enough clues so he thought he'd got away with his stalling tactics. 'I did the shopping but I might be late bringing it over.'

Another pause. At this stage he usually still got her confused with Rachel, the carer who called in on him. 'Oh, right.'

'Have you got enough food in to last you until this evening?'

'Oh ... yes,' he replied, unsure.

'Go to the kitchen cupboard for me. The one with my photo above it.' She'd positioned it there last year and now she used it as a reference every time she called. She heard him walk out of the hall and into the kitchen.

'Yes. Leah. Yes. How are you?'

He'd seen it. Knew who she was. 'I'm fine. Just let me know what you've got in the cupboard.'

'And how is—'

'Elliot.' She didn't have time to let him remember on his own. 'He's fine.' Her father didn't know that they were in the process of separating. And she couldn't possibly tell him what was going on now. Her father used to be the one she could always turn to when life got on top of her. 'Just tell me what you've got there. Plenty of tins?'

'Oh yes ... Elliot.'

'Are there enough tins to open, if you get hungry?'

'Yes. I've had my dinner,' he answered irritably, as if she were fussing over nothing.

She wondered if he'd even had breakfast. 'As long as you don't forget to eat. I'll be over as soon as I can, OK?'

'Yes, yes, yes...' he said dismissively. 'Is your sister coming too?'

Normally, his mention of Olivia was guaranteed to upset her. Olivia had been nine when she'd died. But today she had no time for the pain. 'No, it'll just be me.'

'I haven't seen Leah for an age either,' he said conspiratorially. He'd clearly forgotten that he was talking to her and that she'd been there the previous Saturday, like she was every week.

'I'll be there as quick as I can, Dad.'

There was another gap as he absorbed that. 'Yes, I know.' He sounded angry now.

'Have something to eat.'

'I've told you, I've just eaten!' He hung up on her.

Leah was approaching the railway station. There was a row of cabs waiting outside. She picked up her pace, quickly crossed the road and opened the door of the one at the front of the line.

Reggae poured out from the interior but the young man with dreads was pasty white.

He smiled at her, flashing a gold tooth.

Leah thought he wasn't much older than twenty.

'Where you headed?'

It was a good question.

Chapter Thirty-One

Leah almost shut the door again but then dropped into the seat. 'Forley ... please.' Where else could she go? Would Martin Tate expect her to return there? It was the last place she'd seen Elliot.

The driver seemed oblivious to her indecision and started the engine.

Leah closed her door and he pulled out into the traffic. 'D'you mind turning that down?'

The driver adjusted the volume, but it sounded the same as before.

What would she do when she got there? All that seemed important was putting distance between her and the police. She twisted to look out of the rear window at the cars behind them.

'Being followed?' the driver asked jokingly.

She turned to the front again but didn't respond, keeping her eye on the wing mirror.

Was she really going to wait for a message while Elliot was in danger? But what could the police do in the meantime? They could trace a call though. Maybe that was the only way to find out where he'd been taken. *Turn around. Go back.*

Leah clutched her overnight bag tightly in her lap. She looked down and saw her knuckles white around the straps.

'Sure nobody's after you?' But this time the driver didn't sound so jovial. He eyed the bag.

'Just in a hurry.'

He nodded, unconvinced, and returned his attention to the road.

But she wasn't in a hurry. When she got out the other end, she didn't have the slightest idea what she was going to do.

It seemed only a few seconds between them leaving Middleton and the cab heading back down Plough Lane. It felt like a lifetime ago that she'd hit the deer there, but it was less than twenty-four hours.

As they rounded the bend, Leah was dismayed to see that the animal still hadn't been removed.

'Whoah.' The driver swerved around it.

Leah registered that it had been glanced by other cars and that its increasingly battered carcass had been turned to a different position.

As they passed it, she recalled its last misty breath trailing away into the darkness.

'Poor fella.' The driver regarded the animal in his rear-view.

Leah kept silent, surveyed the right side of the road. She could make out the tyre marks she'd made by the overhanging briers and up ahead she could see there were still two patrol cars, Elliot's Vauxhall and a large white van outside Alice Booth's house. Were they removing the body?

Leah's phone rang. She quickly took it out and checked the screen.

ELLIOT

She answered and clasped it to her left ear so it was furthest away from the driver.

'Leah.' It *was* him, whispering.

'Are you all right?'

'Are you alone?' His voice sounded strange, echoey. Was he on speaker?

'Yes. Just … I'm heading home in a cab.'

'I can only talk to you alone,' he gasped.

'What's happening? Where are you?'

'Alone.' He barely squeezed out the word.

'Pull over.' Leah told the driver.

'What for?'

'This is where I want to get out.'

'I can't drop you here. It's a main road.'

'Come on, the traffic's stopping at the lights.' She indicated the line of cars decelerating in front of them.

'You said Forley.'

Leah produced her credit card. 'Charge me double. Just let me out.'

The driver slowed to a standstill, quickly scanned the

card and Leah was out of the vehicle as soon as he handed it back to her.

'Stand on the other side of the road!' he yelled after her.

The car behind beeped as she carried her bag over to the grass bank.

'Are you still there?' Leah pressed the phone hard to her ear as engines accelerated. She stepped up onto the bank. She was about fifty yards from the police cars outside Alice Booth's house.

An inaudible gasp from Elliot.

'Elliot!'

'How did it go with the police?' He choked out the words.

'What's happening? Where are you?'

'Just answer the question,' he hissed.

'I told them nothing.' Her bag dropped onto the grass.

'You mustn't. Promise me.'

Was Tate listening? 'I promise. I promise. They took me to the park and then the station. I got out of there as soon as I could. They don't know about the texts.'

Again Elliot became incoherent, sounded like he was struggling for air.

'Don't touch him!' she yelled over the cars.

Silence.

Had the phone been hung up? 'Elliot? Elliot?'

But she could still hear the atmosphere, discerned a sliding sound and then an impact on the mouthpiece.

'Answer me. Elliot?'

The next voice was a familiar one. And it was still calm

and accommodating. 'Leah Talbot, you have to let me explain.'

Chapter Thirty-Two

Leah took another step back from the traffic and felt sharp branches against her back. Martin Tate's breath lightly boomed against her ear and it seemed to blow cold inside her. 'Please, don't harm him.'

'We're just getting to know each other.' There wasn't a trace of humour in the response. He said it defensively, as if she'd somehow interrupted.

She managed to swallow and moisten her throat. 'Why are you doing this?'

'I needed to know more about the man you married.'

She ignored the implications of that. 'Please, let him go. I did as you asked. I didn't mention your messages to the police.'

'But you've spent half the day with them. How did that happen?'

'They were there when I went back to Alice Booth's house.'

'Why did you go there?'

165

'To give you a gift.'

A pause. 'What did you bring me?'

'A bottle of wine.'

'That's most thoughtful but really unnecessary.' It sounded like what he would have said if things had gone as she'd envisioned that morning. If he'd answered the door. If it had actually been his home.

'The police started asking me questions.'

'Sorry. I was surprised they were on the case so soon.' He sounded genuinely apologetic. 'I didn't mean for you to go through that.'

'That's ... OK.' Leah wanted to scream at him. A sane person couldn't hold the sort of conversation they were having.

'When you left the umbrella behind, I was convinced you wouldn't come back.'

'I just wanted to say thank you. That was all.' She fought to keep her voice steady.

'Did the police say how they came to be summoned to the house?' he asked, casually.

'The cleaner let herself in.'

No response.

Was he chiding himself for the mistake? 'I only told the police what happened. I've done as you said since.'

'They wanted you to point me out at the park.' It was a statement not a question.

'Yes.' She knew he'd been there but how close?

'I wasn't ever going to hand myself in. I needed to see the people who are looking for me. Put a face to a name. Who's in charge of the investigation?'

'DI Byrne.'

'Is she treating you OK?'

So he'd seen her. 'Yes. When are you going to let Elliot go?'

'I haven't decided.' He suddenly sounded irritable.

Leah had to keep him on the phone. 'Is he OK?'

'He's fine,' he answered dismissively, as if Elliot was an irrelevance.

'Can I speak to him?'

'Did you speak to him last night?'

'When I got home?'

'Yes. On Valentine's Day. After you'd spent the night fending for yourself on a dangerous road. You had a chance then. Did you talk about me?'

Leah wondered what Elliot was making of their exchange. 'Yes.'

'What did you tell him?'

'I told him everything that happened.' But she knew where he was headed.

'Everything?'

'Yes.'

A short silence. 'And you told him you were driving over to see me this morning?'

'No.'

'Why not?' He almost spoke over her answer.

'Please, just let him go.'

'I don't think he knows.'

'About what?'

'About us.'

Leah felt the sibilance of his last word slither over her.

'There is no us.' But Leah regretted her reply as soon as she'd said it.

'I think somebody's deluding themselves.'

'Where are you holding Elliot?'

'I told you, he's fine,' he sounded irked again. 'I'll let you speak to him again soon.'

'Why not now?'

'Because now *we're* in the middle of having a conversation. And it's probably better for Elliot, and certainly less awkward for you, if he earwigs what we're saying and draws his own conclusions. It's going to be tough for him. But this has to happen sooner or later.'

Chapter Thirty-Three

'What's going to be tough for Elliot?' Leah demanded.

'From his expression I would say he already knows.'

Leah closed her eyes so she could focus on their conversation. 'I'll do anything. Just let him go.'

'Anything?'

'Yes.' She nodded abstractedly, tried to block out the stream of traffic.

'Have you any concept of what that could mean?'

'Just tell me what you want.'

'You clearly value Elliot, even if he doesn't value you.'

Leah guessed his loud reply was for Elliot's benefit. Was he bound? 'I promise, I won't tell the police.'

'But what have you already told them?'

'Just … what happened last night.'

'So you described me?'

'Yes.' There was no point in her lying about that.

'Did you tell them that you kissed me?'

Leah clenched her jaw. Imagined Elliot listening in.

'What do you think would have happened if you'd completely succumbed to the moment?'

'I didn't.'

'Did Elliot ask you where you'd been last night or did he not care?'

'Let me speak to him.'

'If you hadn't come home, would he even have cared then?'

'Yes.' But Leah knew what the real answer was.

'Or was he only thinking about the woman who dropped him off?'

Leah stiffened. Tate had obviously waited outside after he'd left the house. Watched her husband as her neighbours had.

'Did you know about Katya?'

'Yes.' But she hadn't until today. And now she had her name. It wasn't one she recognised.

'Attractive girl. And so convenient for Elliot.'

Leah recalled how the Trents had said she'd walked away after she'd dropped Elliot off.

'Three streets from your marital home.' He raised his voice again, for his prisoner's sake.

Leah could hear an incoherent exclamation. It was Elliot. 'What did you do?' Dread billowed inside her.

'19a Medford Avenue. First-floor apartment. Nice place.'

Elliot was shouting against whatever covered his mouth.

'So, you see, you shouldn't have felt any guilt this morning. About anything you did last night.'

'What did you do?' Leah articulated the question that she knew Elliot was struggling to yell.

'I could send you a photo.'

Elliot screamed louder.

'But there's already photos on your phone you probably still haven't looked at.'

Leah froze. She had to open the archive but kept the handset pinned to her ear. What pictures had been sitting there all day?

'Might be worth taking a look at those first.'

Leah couldn't hear the cars now. 'Tell me what you did.' But she could hear a thudding sound, like the feet of a metal chair rocking against a stone floor.

'Go and call on Katya. I wonder how many times Elliot's been up and down her flight of stairs?'

'Stop this now.' But Leah already knew he wasn't about to.

'I'll give you half an hour. Then I'll call you again. Can you remember the address?'

'Yes.' She knew the road.

'I wonder if Elliot would be quite so frantic if it was you in that apartment.'

Momentarily, she recalled how cold Elliot had been when she'd told him about the collision.

'He does seem very agitated right now. I'll calm him down.'

Leah heard the thudding sound getting louder. 'Don't touch him.'

'After what he's been up to? That's very reasonable.'

'This has nothing to do with you!'

'Half an hour. Will that be enough time?'

'I'll go!' She dragged in a breath.

'We'll talk soon.'

'Wait! Stay on the line!'

But he'd cut the call.

Chapter Thirty-Four

L eah immediately hit redial and got an answering service. 'Call me back. I'm not going anywhere until I've spoken with Elliot.' She hung up and waited, blood rushing through her ears. She felt utterly isolated.

No response. She redialled the number. Answering service. She hung up again. Tate was clearly ignoring her and she was wasting time. *Start walking*.

If he wasn't going to pick up, better to make for where she'd been sent. She didn't want to be spotted by the police at Alice Booth's though. Leah left her overnight bag where it was, traversed the grass bank and waited for a gap in the cars. While she did, she quickly opened her photo archive.

Her breath caught in her throat as soon as she saw the last clutch of images. It was her lying on the floor in Alice Booth's kitchen, her features oblivious. She flicked back through them, the angles changing. He'd got right up close to her face with her camera.

A wave of repulsion broke through her as she imagined

him crouching over her. What had been going through Tate's mind as he'd taken them? Had he always planned for her to find them later or had he still not made his mind up about letting her go then? There was no time to consider that now. She had to focus on what she'd been told to do. There seemed little point in calling him back.

The traffic briefly ebbed, and she crossed the road, quickly trotted to the other side and headed for the lights.

A few minutes later, a handful of cars had beeped angrily at her but she'd made it there and turned left onto the path that ran beside the road and led to the roundabout on the outskirts of Forley. She tried not to think of what was waiting for her in the upstairs apartment. *Concentrate on each individual step.*

She went straight ahead at the roundabout. She could avoid town and take a left that would lead her to the top of Medford Avenue. But when she reached the turning, she froze. What was she walking into?

A couple pushing a pram walked by her and she vaguely registered their expressions shift from smiles to concern as they passed her. She was standing in the corner gutter staring down the road.

She was about to walk into the home of Elliot's lover. Her obvious fear aside, shouldn't she consider what she might find and what conclusions would be drawn from her presence there? But she had no choice. The police were out of the equation and she had to think only of Elliot's safety.

Leah strode on, checking the number on her left. 110. The house would be on the right towards the end of the road. She crossed over and it felt like a hand was clenching her windpipe.

There were no other pedestrians in sight and a plane boomed overhead. But the sound seemed to continue resonating through her as she reached the door of number 19. It was glass and she peered through to the shared hallway beyond. Two white front doors for 19 and 19a.

Leah pulled on the handle, but the door was locked. Beside her were two buttons. The top one said M Wilson, the one below K Boyers. There was an intercom grill. She gulped and jabbed the one for K Boyers.

There was no sound when she did so, but she waited, her eyes fixed on the grill. *Please, let a woman's voice answer.*

No response.

Leah pressed the button again. Harder and longer this time.

Still nothing.

What was she meant to do if she couldn't get inside? Did Tate expect her to break in? She took out her phone and dialled his number again. Answering service.

Leah tried the other button.

'Yes?' A male voice answered brusquely.

Leah wondered how to proceed. 'Hello. I'm trying to get hold of Katya.'

'Who?' He sounded half asleep.

'The girl who lives upstairs from you.'

'What's that got to do with me?'

'She's expecting me,' Leah lied. 'But I can't raise her. I think she said her bell is on the blink. Can you just let me in so I can knock on her door?'

'Can't you just phone her?'

Leah thought on her feet. 'I'm not charged up.'

There was no reply but a few seconds later, the door buzzed.

Leah pushed on it and found herself in the small hallway that smelt strongly of varnish. The front door harshly slammed behind her. Now what? The door to 19a was firmly locked. She knocked three times on it, more for the benefit of the neighbour who had let her in.

She waited, her mind suddenly blank.

'Hello?' A muffled woman's voice said.

Leah was briefly confused then realised it was coming from the intercom. She opened the front door again and spoke into the grill. 'Hello?' She held the door open with her hand.

'Just a minute, I'll be down now,' the woman said.

The intercom clunked off and Leah returned to the hallway.

A moment later, there were thuds on the stairs.

Leah stood back and her body tensed.

The door clicked as it was unlocked and then opened inwards. A tall, pale-skinned girl with her fair hair pinned into a lazy bun on her head was standing there. 'Are you OK?' She spoke when she realised Leah wasn't about to.

'I'm Leah.'

Nothing registered in the girl's eyes.

'Elliot's wife.'

A half frown evaporated as realisation sunk in.

At that point Leah acknowledged that the girl was wearing a familiar green top and trousers. The word

'Gleason's' was written in yellow on her breast. It was the local garden centre and she was clearly on her way into work.

But Leah had already bypassed the emotions that she should have felt. She was just glad the girl hadn't been harmed.

'Um...' She looked awkward and then turned away from Leah and shouted up the stairs. 'Katya! Somebody here to see you!'

Chapter Thirty-Five

Thirteen hours earlier

Having just left Leah Talbot in the shower, Tate turned right out of her driveway and was about to return to his Nissan when he heard a car coming along the street. Its headlights extended along the road before him and he realised he would soon be lit up. Trotting across the tarmac he made for the cover of a tree and its shadow the other side.

Standing behind the trunk, he shrank back further as the vehicle slowed and pulled into Leah Talbot's driveway. So Elliot was home at last. But as he watched from his hiding place, he could see there were two people in the car, one male, one female.

The male occupant, who Tate assumed was Elliot, got out of the passenger side first and looked up at the house. He was holding a paper bag of what looked like takeout food.

The female got out of the driver's side. She was slim and had bleached-blonde hair. Dark fur coat and high black boots. Who was this?

Elliot, who was shorter than he'd imagined, bounced nervously on his feet while he waited for the woman to move around the car towards him.

'Is she back?' the woman asked.

They were both whispering but he could hear them perfectly.

'Looks like it.' Elliot pushed his hands in his pockets.

'Why don't we *both* go inside?' she suggested, nervous determination in her voice.

'No, not like this.'

Her shoulders sagged a little. 'It's not going to be easy, whenever we do it.'

'I'm drunk. It's not the right time.' His body was stiff.

'I'll be with you.' She reached out to him.

How old was she? Early twenties at the most?

He flinched from her touch. 'You said you wouldn't pressure me.'

She retracted her hand. 'It's been sixteen months. I wouldn't call that pressure.'

Elliot shifted his attention back to the windows.

'If she gets ugly, you can come and stay at my place.'

'She won't get ugly.' Elliot seemed sure of that.

'Then what's stopping you? She's got to know you're moving on. When you do, she will too.'

'She will. But this isn't the way.'

'When then?' Exasperation raised her voice.

'Quiet. She'll hear.'

Elliot's companion sighed.

'Look, thanks for the lift. I'll call you tomorrow.'

'Call me when you're in bed.'

'OK,' he conceded.

'Unless you're still sleeping with her.'

He breathed slowly in. 'Katya, how many times do we have to go over this?'

'Then why don't you tell her?'

'I've told you, sorting out all our joint policies is going to be easier if she isn't trying to kill me.'

'You said she wouldn't get ugly.'

'She won't. Just…'

'Give you a little more time?'

He turned his head to the upstairs windows again. 'Let's talk about it on the phone. Not here.'

She looked down at the toes of her high black boots.

'Look, I'll see you tomorrow.' He waited.

She nodded then looked up again and put her arms around his neck.

Elliot stiffened as she kissed him hard.

Tate guessed she wanted Leah to catch them.

Eventually she let him go and then strutted off without another word.

He'd been expecting Elliot's companion to get back in the car and pushed himself against the shadowy wall behind him.

She turned out of the driveway and strode up the street.

Elliot watched her go, faltered up to the front door, fumbled out his keys and then went inside the house.

Tate remained in the shadows because something else

had caught his eye. Somebody was standing in the bedroom window of next door. He'd clearly been woken by Elliot's and the girl's conversation. Or had he been watching longer? The man talked to a woman behind him and then closed the blinds.

When he was sure the neighbour wasn't going to make another appearance, he turned his head in the direction of Katya's receding footsteps. So Elliot was cheating on Leah. And had been for sixteen months. And, it appeared, with someone right on their doorstep. But how close?

He regarded the quiet house before him. Part of him was relieved they were sleeping separately. Or had that been a lie for Katya's benefit? But Leah's comment about Valentine's night said otherwise. He felt buoyed by the image of Leah showered and tucked up alone. Didn't sound like Elliot was going to rush into any confessions tonight.

He headed off after Katya, picking up his pace and then slowing as she came into view on the other side of the street. He followed her at a distance for four minutes as she cut left down two side streets and then scrabbled in her handbag outside a glass front door.

He hung back as she produced her keys and went up the short pathway. He stole across the road, checking the darkened windows of the houses either side. But when his attention shifted back to Katya she had turned from the door and was looking directly at him.

'Are you following me?'

He paused, halfway across the road.

'Well?'

'Yes.' He intended to wrongfoot her with an honest answer.

She was briefly speechless.

'I can't deny it.' His brain sped ahead of his mouth. 'My name's Martin Tate.'

She raised her palm as he took another step forward. 'Just stay where you are.'

'I won't have to. This is effectively the end of my shift. My fault not yours though.'

She frowned.

'I'm employed by Leah Talbot. I'm a private investigator.'

She didn't react.

'Now you've spotted me, there's little point in me hanging around. But, full disclosure, I think I already have enough.'

'She's hired you to follow me?' she asked, incredulous.

'No. To follow Mr Talbot. But he led me to you.'

He could see her turn this over. A smirk eventually broke over her face.

'I'm so sorry if I frightened you.'

She shook her head but was deep in thought. 'No, that's OK.'

'And I hope you don't take this personally. It's a job. A shitty one sometimes but it's a job.'

'So, you'll be reporting back to her?'

'Yes. I'm afraid so.'

She waved her hand. 'Don't worry about it. You'll be calling her in the morning, I suppose?'

He looked at his watch. 'Yes, a little late now.'

'OK. Goodnight,' she said abruptly, turned her back on him and opened her front door.

He knew she was off to phone Elliot to warn him right away. She didn't even look back. If she had she would have seen him coming up the pathway behind her and slipping on his blue gloves. She'd seen his face.

Silencing her, threatening her and getting her through the door to her apartment was easy.

Unfortunately, ten minutes later, as he laid out his razor blades and prepared to complete his work, he had to cut things short when he heard her roommate come home.

Chapter Thirty-Six

'You're not Katya?' Leah had to stand to one side as the girl pushed by her.

'No. I just work two jobs and pay her rent,' she replied caustically before opening the front door.

'Should I just go up?'

She turned, a look of sadistic satisfaction on her face. 'Make yourself at home. She's still asleep. Doesn't usually get up until mid-afternoon but feel free to go in and wake her.' A trace of sympathy registered in her expression. 'I'm glad she's not just my problem.'

'You know who I am?'

The girl nodded once. 'You're not the first marriage she's ruined,' she whispered, then glanced back up the stairs, as if afraid to be overheard. 'Last door on the left,' she hissed then headed out of the front door.

Leah was left looking up the faded crimson carpeted stairs. The door slammed shut behind her. She could now hear the muted TV from behind the door to number 19 over the clamour in her head.

Climbing the stairs two at a time she was greeted by the aroma of coffee at the top. Leah was standing on a long landing with white doors leading off. At the end she could see through the open door to the kitchen. Pots, pans and plates were stacked up in the sink under the window. She could hear the slow rhythm of a tap dripping onto the frying pan.

The last door on the left was shut. Leah padded down the faded runner, but the boards creaked as she approached. She paused outside the door. She could see right into the compact and spartan kitchen now. A dirty plate and a coffee mug were sitting on a small dining table in the corner. A single cafetiere steamed beside the draining board.

What should she do? Knock? Storm in? Leah leaned close to the panel. 'Katya?' Her voice was hoarse. 'Katya,' she repeated louder.

No response or movement from behind the door.

'Katya,' she stated the name flatly. But it suddenly struck Leah that the girl that shared with her hadn't said she'd seen Katya. 'Katya,' she declared more urgently and knocked on the wood.

Still no reply.

Leah turned the cold brass knob and pushed in. A heavy scent of sweet perfume wafted over her. The room was in darkness, only a slim bar of daylight bisected the heavy curtains.

Should she turn on the light? Leah looked beside her for a switch but couldn't see one.

From the illumination spilling in from the landing she could make out a shape under the dark duvet. 'Katya?' She didn't want to drag the girl from the bed to confront her. Only one thing was important.

Leah approached the bed and could see the girl's long bleached hair lying across the pillow. Her face was turned to the wall. She opened her mouth to say her name again but thought better of it.

She'd reached the mattress and Leah registered a number of pill canisters on the shelf over the bedstead. She waited, listened for the sound of the girl's breathing.

Please be alive.

There was no sound. No movement of the duvet rising and falling. Momentarily, Leah was back at the roadside, waiting for the deer's breath.

She extended her hand to the duvet and the material felt cold in her hot palm. 'Katya.' It was her last warning. Leah wanted the girl to jump in fright, to emerge bleary-eyed from the bed and demand to know who she was.

She pulled the duvet back in one movement, exposing all of Katya's foetal position. She was naked and Leah could see a long dark snake tattoo across the shoulder nearest to her.

Leah knew she was dead before she turned her. Her fingers gripped her cold shoulder and her body resisted, stiffly.

She had to see her face. She found herself kneeling on the edge of the mattress, both her hands on the woman's arm so she could roll her towards her. She still wouldn't turn. Leah used more force.

The body gave but the face that lolled towards her on the pillow had a piece of cloth stuffed in its mouth. Katya's cheeks bulged with it and her bulbous open eyes did the same. Looked like a pair of nylon tights had been stuffed inside. There was a black belt around her throat. The buckle was secured tight and the leather appeared to be embedded in her pale skin. Saliva had dribbled out of her mouth and streaked her chin.

Leah recognised the gold buckle. It was the belt Martin Tate had been wearing when he'd let her in to Alice Booth's. She pushed herself away and stumbled back.

The edge of the open bedroom door struck her spine but she didn't feel the pain. A scream was building inside her. Leah couldn't take her eyes from the woman on the bed, her legs bent up and her arms stiff, the wrists curved and fingers turned in towards her chest.

Leah emitted a sound but didn't know if it was a sob or a retch of repulsion. She was on the landing again, her back against the wall there and her gaze still on Katya. She'd never seen a dead body before.

A motorbike buzzed noisily by in the street outside and her face eventually turned in its direction. She was looking into the kitchen again, her attention on the window. Everything outside was normal. Nothing inside was.

The tap continued to drip onto the frying pan.

Dazed, Leah turned back to the stairs. What was she supposed to do now? She remained against the wall, her attention fixed there but her feet not obeying her brain.

Leave. Go. Move.

With Elliot's life threatened, Leah couldn't call the police but she couldn't just walk away from Katya. She trotted quickly back into the bedroom and pulled the duvet back over her body. Only her hair was visible above it now.

Leah could smell the girl's perfume even more strongly now. It was overpowering.

How old was she? Who were her parents? Did she have a brother or sister?

She started to choke on the cloying aroma as one truth presented itself to her. If Leah hadn't stopped at Alice Booth's place, nobody would have followed her to her house. And then nobody would have followed Katya home.

Chapter Thirty-Seven

L eah pulled the door to 19a shut but it didn't close. She slid her fingers under the metal tab below the keyhole and tried again, but it still wouldn't lock. Beside her she could vaguely hear the TV muttering in number 19. She pushed the door all the way open so she could get a full swing and had a third attempt. The door still came to rest awkwardly in the frame. A harder yank didn't make any difference. 'Come on!' she growled, aware that the man in the downstairs flat would probably hear.

The door clicked into place on the fifth attempt.

Leah could feel her heart knocking against her chest as she opened the front door and walked outside. She was glad of the cool fresh air on her face but Katya's perfume still lingered about her.

How could she possibly leave Katya for her roommate to find when she got home? She looked up and down the street, but she was long gone. How long had Leah been inside, a handful of minutes? She inhaled sharply through her nose and checked the downstairs window, expecting to see a man looking out.

But the navy-blue curtains were closed. It didn't matter if he saw her though. Katya's roommate seemed to know exactly who she was.

She recalled the strangled sound Elliot had made during Tate's phone call to her and the warning she'd been given. Leah couldn't report Katya's murder to the police. Not yet.

She found herself back in the street. A refuse collection lorry was working its way down from the end that Leah had entered. Which direction should she go? She took out her phone and tried dialling Elliot's number again. Answering service.

She turned and looked up at the window. She could see the handle of the frying pan sticking up at the bottom of the kitchen pane and imagined the drip of the tap still thudding and Katya's covered and motionless body on the mattress.

Bottles clunked and crashed as the refuse men got closer and Leah tried to focus on anything but what she'd just left behind her. *What now?* She had to go but didn't know where.

The phone buzzed harshly in her hand.

'Hello?'

There was a long pause. 'Olivia?' It was her father.

'No, it's Leah. Dad, I really can't talk at the moment.'

Another pause, as if he were chewing over the name. 'Leah, Rachel hasn't arrived. I'm getting worried.'

'Rachel isn't due to call in this afternoon. I am.'

'I know,' he improvised.

'Look, I'm going to have to go.'

'What time will you be here? I was going to have a shower.'

'Go ahead and have it.' But it was something he seldom did. 'Just be careful. I'll be there as soon as possible.' But when would that be?

'OK. I'll be out by the time you're here.'

She kept her eyes on the blue curtains of number 19. It was doubtful her father would remember he was having a shower by the time he'd put down the phone let alone that she was meant to be visiting. 'Why don't you just watch TV until I arrive.'

'Uh...' He considered it. 'Yes, perhaps...'

He could do that for hours. At least Leah knew he was safe while he did that. 'OK, just watch TV until I arrive.' But she was also aware that it only took a small distraction to set him off in another direction. 'I'll be there as soon as I can.' But there was no way she could go there now. What should she do? *Call Rachel.*

'Hurry then.' He sounded impatient and rang off.

Now she was worried that he wouldn't go and watch TV. He'd already had a couple of falls in the bathroom. Leah could feel the situation begin to overwhelm her. Her breathing was shallow and even though the refuse men were getting steadily nearer the noises they were making seemed to be fading. *Hold it together.*

She headed away from them, putting one foot deliberately in front of the other and making her way to the high street end of Medford Avenue. She could see the traffic moving fast there but the situation seemed so unreal. She phoned Rachel but got her answering service. She was walking away from a dead body. But she had to if she wanted Elliot back. Where was he now? What was Tate doing to him?

The phone vibrated again.

'Talking to someone?' Tate sounded irritated.

Leah stopped dead. 'My father called me.'

'You're sure?'

'He's got Alzheimer's. He calls all the time.'

'I won't call back again if you're on the phone.'

'I'm sorry. He calls all the time,' she repeated.

'Where are you?'

'I've been into Katya's place.' Just uttering her name brought the image of her last expression back. Her body started to tremble. 'I saw what you did...' Leah's voice quivered too.

'You spoke to her?'

'What are you talking about?' She tightened her grip on the phone, as if it could halt the tremor of her legs.

'Good. I hope you didn't give her too hard a time. Elliot's understandably concerned about the two of you sharing the same space.'

Leah realised what he was doing. Elliot must still be in earshot and he was concealing the fact that he'd killed her.

'I think you two meeting was the best thing that could have happened. I bet she was at a loss for words when you walked in the door. No catfighting, I hope?'

'I did what you asked. Let him go now.'

'Was she sorry?'

Leah didn't answer.

'She pleaded,' he continued, as if he was repeating what Leah had said.

But she guessed he was telling her what Katya had done the night before.

Chapter Thirty-Eight

L eah didn't notice as the refuse collectors passed her.
'Pleading, always uncomfortable to be around.'
He carried on the conversation for Elliot's benefit.

The lorry trundled by.

'Why did you have to kill her?' She spoke low as a man in a high vis jacket weaved around her.

'It had to happen,' he answered simply. 'That situation couldn't continue as it was.'

'You didn't even know her.'

'Now the two of you have become acquainted we have to decide what to do about Elliot next.'

Leah could hear a muted protest from Elliot in the background. Relief was overridden by how weak he sounded. 'What have you done to him?'

'Just a little something to keep him manageable.'

'Why are you doing this to us?'

There was a pause. 'So, you would have been quite happy to carry on as you were?'

'I... Just let me know what you need me to do.' Leah realised it was raining. A droplet landed on her eyelid.

'You know what you have to do. Decide whether you really want him back.'

'Of course I do.'

'Of course you do? So he can cheat on you again?'

'But he didn't. Elliot and I are over.' It was the first time she'd said that.

He hesitated before replying. 'You're saying that now...' But he sounded unsure.

'I'm not. We sleep in separate rooms.' Was this the way to remove Elliot from danger? Did Tate see him as a rival to be erased?

'You knew he was seeing Katya?'

'Yes.' Then she responded to the silence that followed. 'I knew he was seeing somebody. But he was free to. We only live together for convenience now.'

'Is that why you weren't spending Valentine's together?'

'Yes.' Leah waited as he assessed what she'd told him.

'You have no feelings for him, and he has no feelings for you?'

'Not anymore.' She had to convince him of that.

'So whatever I do to him means nothing to you?'

'Of course it does.'

'Why?'

'I don't want him harmed,' she said emphatically.

Elliot grunted and she could hear the chair legs knocking again.

'What about Katya? Even though you'd never seen her face until today...'

Leah would never forget her stuffed expression.

'You didn't wish *her* dead?'

'No.' Anger filled out her reply.

'I wonder if Elliot will. When he tries to look past the sex and realises she's just too young for him and considers all the complications that they've got ahead of them. D'you think he'll wish her dead?'

'Nobody deserves to die like that.'

'You forget. I've seen you with blood on your hands.'

'That was an animal. An accident.' Was that why he'd spared her at the house?

'That's twice I've helped you now.'

She shivered but it was nothing to do with the cold rain running down her face. 'If you really want to help me, let Elliot go.'

'I can't do that. You know that.'

Leah felt the ground tilt. 'Why not?'

'He's seen me. Like Katya did.'

She closed her eyes. 'Let him go ... for me.'

'"Let him go"? Sounds like something you should have done a long time ago.'

'You're right.' She had to find a way inside his warped logic. 'I think I began to do that when I came to see you this morning.'

He thought about that. 'And you came to see *me*?'

'Yes.'

'You've not been with another man outside of your marriage?'

'No.' She would tell him anything he needed to know, however private. Anything to keep him from hurting Elliot.

'I believe something conspired to bring you to the house last night.' He seemed certain of that. 'I had to open up. Even though I could so easily have left you out there.'

Why did he answer the door? Katya would still be alive, and Leah would still be in ignorance of her. And Elliot would be safe.

'I looked down at you from the window and recognised you immediately.'

Leah opened her eyes.

'I'd watched you. Two days before. And four days before that. How could I not let you in?'

Chapter Thirty-Nine

'First time, I sat four feet away from you in Langtry's.'

But Leah was listening for Elliot. The sound of the rocking chair had stopped.

'You were side on. Didn't register me. You ordered a cinnamon latte. I played a game. Tried to put a name to your face. But then they called it out and you collected your coffee from the counter. Just sat there stirring it. You were so deep in thought. I had to speculate why.'

'I did what you asked. Let me speak to him.'

'I'd come to the area a week before I called on Alice. Langtry's was ideal because they don't have any security cameras in there like they do in the pub.'

'Please,' she whispered.

'Answer me one question first. What was it that you were thinking about?'

'I don't remember.'

'The second time. Thursday. You did the same. Plain latte instead though.'

She felt cold creep over her as she saw herself sitting obliviously at her usual table with his eyes planted on her. She really hadn't seen him, on either occasion. But he was right, she had been lost in her thoughts. 'I really don't know.'

'But it was only a few days ago. Lunchtime. You didn't eat anything.'

'I had a lot on my mind.'

'So I guessed. I envisioned all kinds of scenarios. Were you thinking about Elliot?'

'Yes. Please put him on.'

'Right then, I wouldn't have believed a woman like you could have been jilted.'

'I have to know he's OK.' She still couldn't hear him.

'You still haven't answered my question.'

'I told you. I was thinking about him.'

'Specifically?'

Leah knew she had to be careful. She couldn't tell him of the thoughts she'd really entertained. That she still felt they had a chance. That would endanger Elliot. Tate clearly saw him as a threat to dispose of. 'I've been seeing a counsellor. I'd had my final session with her that week.'

'A relationship counsellor?'

'Yes.'

'You said "I". Does that mean Elliot didn't?'

'No.'

'Why not?'

'He refused to.'

'Shouldn't that tell you everything you need to know? If

Elliot didn't want to attend, then he must have had no interest in salvaging your relationship.'

'It was that day I decided it was time for me to move on.' It was a lie. She'd still wanted to work things out. She hadn't known about Katya. But she couldn't even intimate that. 'I've answered your question. Let him go.'

'After all he's done. Have you forgotten Katya?'

How could she ever?

'He's betrayed you.' He sounded exasperated. 'He can't go unpunished for that.'

Leah could hear the hostility in his voice building. She had to misdirect him. 'What about Alice Booth? Did she deserve to be punished too?'

There was a pause. 'That was a personal transaction.'

What the hell did that mean? 'You knew her?'

'Long time ago. Reminded her exactly who I was just before she died.'

Leah felt sickened that he spoke of her death as if it was something he'd simply been present at and wasn't responsible for.

'She seemed understandably perplexed when I told her. Alice has been through two divorces since we last clapped eyes on each other.'

Leah had to know. 'Why did you kill her?'

'She was like an entirely different person last night. Did you know that after seven to ten years every cell in the human body is replaced? That means that Alice had become a whole new person three times over since I last saw her.'

Leah remained silent.

'There was no anger. On my part. And you need that bypass when you kill someone. You can't allow emotions to cloud what you do. It's a lot harder than people think so I always look upon it as a transaction. Like it was with Katya. I was able to remain removed because I did it for you.'

Leah shuddered to her core. 'No, you didn't.' Leah wouldn't allow him to make her complicit.

'Alice was a personal transaction for me. But for the me of thirty-one years ago. I made myself a promise then. A promise I kept. I've done it three times before. Alice was to be my fourth and last.'

How could she begin to navigate a deranged rationale like that? 'So what did Alice Booth ever do to you?'

'She was only in her late teens. She didn't really know how intense my feelings had been for her then. She had an inkling, but she didn't really know to what extent she inverted my world when she spurned me. I tried to remember my teenage rage when I cut up her face. Not to use it as a spur but to remind myself why I was there. I couldn't summon it though. Not that it's important. Physical vandalism has to be part of the transaction; scoring their faces makes them less human to me. I was just about to do the same to Katya when her friend came home. If she'd seen my face, I would have had to put her in the bed with Katya as well. I always see my commitments through. That's what Alice Booth was. When I was seventeen I promised myself if I didn't find somebody, I'd go and find her. Impact her existence as she had mine. I'd reached a point in my life when I firmly believed there was no one in the world for me. Then I saw you in Langtry's. And as soon as Alice died you were knocking on the front door. I saw what was in your eyes when we were alone. We both felt that connection. That's why I have to make a new commitment to you.'

Chapter Forty

L eah turned her back to a couple walking by her. 'There is no connection between us.' She regretted the words before she'd finished uttering them.

'You can't possibly say that.' He sounded genuinely mortified. 'Not after what's happened in such a short space of time.'

'We only met last night. It was a coincidence.'

'You really believe that?'

'If you really do want to do something for me ... let Elliot go right now. I promise I won't ever mention any of this to the police.'

'Did you hear that?' Tate talked away from the mouthpiece.

Leah strained her ears but couldn't hear any response.

'She's pleading for your release. Even after the unconscionable way you've treated her.'

A low groan.

Leah felt a surge of relief.

'You must have done something pretty spectacular in a previous life to deserve such loyalty from her.'

Then she could hear Elliot scream.

'Stop!'

But whatever was happening to her husband intensified and the scream curdled.

'Stop it!'

It was suddenly cut short.

'What have you done?' She could hear a low breathing at the other end but wasn't sure if it was Elliot or Tate. The phone clunked and momentarily she thought he'd hung up.

'They say a man's tolerance for pain is higher than a woman's. I think that's nonsense.'

'What have you done?'

'Would you rather it was you? After all the pain he's already put you through?'

Leah wiped the rain from her eyes.

'Would you take his place?'

Leah released a faltering breath.

'You'd really do that for him?'

Her fingers and the phone shook at her ear. 'Yes.'

'And if you had him back, you'd forgive him?'

She couldn't answer that.

'Even though you'll still both be over because his pride wouldn't be able to handle what you did to save him?'

'Yes,' she heard herself say. But what did he really expect her to do to free Elliot?

'Do you know what I did to Alice Booth?'

Leah suddenly realised that the young couple had

halted on the other side of the street. They were both looking back at her with concern.

'Are you OK?' The man mouthed.

She nodded and realised there were tears on her face. 'Just ... just my boyfriend. We're ... in the middle of something.'

The man nodded uncertainly, and the woman made meaningful eye contact with her. They moved off.

'Boyfriend?' Tate repeated.

'Where should I go from here? Tell me,' she spat.

'When I was seventeen, Alice Booth lived in my head. The best version of her, the most pristine, glowing Alice existed for a year inside my skull. But the reality was disappointing. I hope you won't disappoint me.'

Leah watched the couple walking away from her, felt the abhorrence for him souring in her throat.

'There were three others. They all promised something to me they never delivered. But Alice was my first. That's why I left her 'til last. That's why I took my time. And when it was done, I felt emptied out. I knew that moment had always been coming and I was just wondering what there was left for me afterwards, when you knocked on the door. Right at that very moment. The girl who had intrigued me. Was I wrong to believe there was some significance in that?'

Leah had no idea how to respond. If she said no, would that endanger Elliot even more?

'Even after our intimate moment, do you still insist there's no connection?'

She had to think fast. 'I can't talk to you properly here ... in the street.'

'But if there's nothing between us, why would you want to talk to me at all? Just to save Elliot's miserable skin?'

'What you say is true. You seeing me. Me coming to the house just as ... you were looking for a new purpose...'

He didn't reply, let her continue.

'Maybe this is all too much for me to process.'

'I can see why that would be.' But his tone was cold.

'Let me come to you.' There was no other way.

'In good time. I still think you need convincing.'

'Of what?'

'Of what you'll need to do. Maybe your neighbours can help.'

'What?'

'The ones who were at the window when I left your house. After I stood outside your bathroom they watched Elliot argue with Katya while I did too.'

Chapter Forty-One

'What are you saying?' Leah felt a sickening jolt and immediately started striding towards the high street.

'Mr and Mrs Trent made the decision to involve themselves.'

'They're nothing to do with this.' She was heading home.

'Exactly the reason they shouldn't have been spying.'

'Please, tell me you didn't harm them.'

'The police are watching your house, but I had no problem getting into the property next door.'

Was this a bluff? When had he come back? After he'd taken Elliot? She'd been with the police for a couple of hours. Her heart and pace quickened.

'Little pathway behind your house and theirs. The back door was open. Should still be. Maybe you can help them out.'

'What did you do?' Leah wanted to yell but kept her

voice low as she passed a family unpacking shopping from a car.

'I was a little pushed for time. Not ideal circumstances for me. I like to be able to inhabit a place. When I work, I prefer not to have any interruptions. Unless it's you, of course.'

Leah was reaching the end of Medford Avenue. She didn't want to cross the busy road to Minster Street, but her legs were propelling her there.

'I'll call you soon.'

'Please, don't hang up.'

But he did.

Leah started to run but had to halt and wait at the roadside as the traffic rolled leisurely by. Darting through a gap in the cars she quickly made it to the other side, jogged by the pub and made for the turning of her street.

She passed Langtry's. If she hadn't walked in there for coffee the same time Tate had, would he have opened the door to her after she'd hit the deer?

The rain eased and she slowed as she got halfway down Minster Street. One or more of the cars parked by the house would have an officer inside. All she had to do was knock on a window and tell them exactly what had happened. That way, she wouldn't have to go into the Trents's house. Would Elliot have a better chance if the police handled it? But Leah was positive the best way of saving his life was doing exactly as she'd been told.

She took a left down a side road, crossed over and spotted the overgrown entrance to the alleyway behind the houses. Would an officer be positioned here? She checked each car as she passed them but none of them were occupied.

Peering through the overgrown reeds that bordered the stream Leah couldn't see if there was anybody waiting there. The track curved around so she could only see as far as the first ten feet or so. She entered the path, the wet weeds on her shins. They swished coldly against her jeans as she strode along the dirt, passing the back gates of each house and slowing as she reached hers.

It was still ajar from Fitch's inspection. She looked in. Everything seemed normal – the overgrown lawn, the unfinished patio and barbecue area. But she felt like an interloper, looking at someone else's home. Someone else's life. She'd only been in the kitchen that morning, gazing out at the long grass, oblivious to everything that had happened and that was about to happen. Leah suddenly seemed so far removed from that moment now.

She passed her garden and came to the Trents's high wooden gate. The dark wood treatment on the panels had faded and had a green mossy sheen. She put her hand to it, wondering if it would be locked. But she could see that there was a dent of exposed orange splinters where it had been booted at the handle. How long ago had he broken in?

She pushed it and revealed the Trents's immaculately kept landscape garden. An ornamental cherry tree was the centrepiece, but it was as bare as every bush that surrounded it. Dark, wet leaves were neatly piled to its right.

Then it occurred to her that Tate could still be here. Could he have called her from inside the house? Her eyes darted about the dark back windowpanes, upstairs and downstairs.

She closed the gate carefully behind her and thought about the police at the front, their attention fixed on the house next door. Leah felt a hand grasping the pit of her stomach, dragging her back as her feet took her along the gravel path.

As she neared their teal, stable door, she could see that it was also ajar. She stopped there, aware of the breath hissing quickly in and out of her nostrils.

She knocked gently on the wood. 'Mr and Mrs Trent?' She could hear the apprehension in her voice.

No answer. Leah could only discern the faint hum of traffic from the high street.

She pushed the door and a warm, inviting aroma rolled out at her. Smelt like home-baked bread. There was nobody in the traditional farmhouse kitchen. The only sound was the low purr of the refrigerator. Wheelback wooden chairs were neatly pushed in at the dining table and there were some fresh flowers laid out on the draining board waiting for a vase.

'Mr and Mrs Trent?' she said louder now she was inside. Leah wanted them to both march into the kitchen. She didn't care if she had to find an explanation for walking into their home, she just wanted them to appear.

Please let this be Tate's sick prank.

But no response came.

Instinct told her to back out now. They'd been in only a few hours earlier. Could they have gone out in the meantime? She cursed herself for not checking that their car had been in their drive when she'd walked into the street at the front. But their hedge would probably have concealed it and she'd have to have looked directly up the driveway and the police would have seen her.

She moved to the stripped door that led to the hallway. 'Mr and Mrs Trent. It's Leah.' But she already knew there'd be no reply. She put her hand on the wooden handle and was about to push it when a noise made her freeze.

It was a low rasping sound.

Leah tilted her ear to the crack. It was definitely coming from the other side of the door ... and nearby.

The noise ceased. Then started again.

Something in the atmosphere was all wrong. Leah's skin tightened as she recalled Katya's vacant expression, tights stuffed into her mouth.

The rasping became more insistent.

Leah kept her breath locked inside her, gripped the handle harder and then pushed the door open.

Chapter Forty-Two

I n the middle of the dark tiled hallway, a ginger cat was sitting licking the underside of its paw.

Leah released a small breath. What was its name? Something to do with *Game of Thrones*. Mr Trent was a big George R. R. Martin fan. She couldn't recall.

The animal straightened its head to regard her properly and then continued what it was doing.

She stepped into the hallway and looked left into the first room she came to. It was a lounge and some magazines were strewn around the tan leather sofa there. Was that sign of a struggle? The Trents seemed pretty fastidious to her. She crossed the threshold and took in her surroundings. One wall was completely covered by bookshelves and there was an antique bureau in the far right corner. No sign of either of them. 'Mr and Mrs Trent? It's Leah from next door.' Her voice sounded very loud and she waited for it to finish echoing around the large room and listened intently.

Nothing.

Leah returned to the hall. The cat paused its cleaning again and tilted its green eyes up to her.

'Hello, puss,' she whispered. But she knew she couldn't allow the cat's nonchalant presence to convince her that everything was as it should be. Leah paced to the next room at the front of the house. Its pine door was closed. 'Let's see if they're in here, shall we?' Leah spoke to the cat so she wouldn't feel she was entirely alone.

Pulling the handle down she released it and allowed the door to swing inwards. This was clearly their formal dining room. A long table with high-backed chairs took up most of the middle floor space and glass-fronted cabinets with antique tureens and platters covered the wall to the rear.

Leah quickly crossed the room and stood a foot from the net curtains in the bay window. She squinted through them at the Kia on the drive. Its presence dismissed any hope that the Trents had gone out. She felt her dread double in weight.

She fixed her gaze upon the vehicle parked on the road opposite the end of the drive. Was it an umarked police car? There was no occupant. Because of the Trents's tall hedge that encompassed the lawn she couldn't see anything more of the street. Maybe they were parked further up. If she needed help it was nearby but it was her house they were focused on, not the one directly next to it.

Was this some sort of trap for her and was she about to discover something worse than she already had?

The cat hissed behind her.

Leah turned back in the direction she'd just come. Nobody had followed her in. She would have heard them.

She tugged open the door to the understairs cupboard and stood swiftly back. Nothing in there but a wall rack of wine bottles.

Her attention shifted to the stairs. She had to go up. But Leah remained where she was, her rapidly beating heart feeling like it was completely filling her chest.

The cat growled, slid past her legs, bounded up the stairs and disappeared. Red light spilled down from the stained-glass window at the top.

'You've got to wait for me.' But she couldn't imbue her voice with anything but fear.

The house was silent.

Leah put her hand on the newel post and slowly started to ascend the dark chocolate carpet on the stairs. She counted them in her head. At fourteen she was at the top and in the middle of a square landing with doors off it. All of them were ajar. The cat had obviously gone through one of them. 'Puss, puss.' She knew the animal wasn't going to return to her.

Leah could smell furniture polish and a floorboard creaked as she readjusted her footing. Had Tate been here? She recalled what he'd said to her on the phone.

I like to be able to inhabit a place.

She fought the reflex to flee. Tate had Elliot with him. He couldn't have brought him to this house. Particularly if he knew the police were watching. But he'd sent her here for a reason.

Leah pushed open the door nearest her. It was a generous office. The Trents were both retired and this was clearly where they ran the household from. Box files were arranged neatly along a shelf and below it was a computer monitor and keyboard. The swivel chair was empty.

The cat meowed.

Leah thought she identified the room it had come from and walked to the door on her right. 'Come on, puss. Where are you?' *Find the cat.*

She pushed the panel hard and the door banged. Was this where the couple slept? There were two single beds next to each other. But there was no clutter on the shelves beside each, so she assumed she was in the guest room.

The cat meowed nearby. This time it echoed.

That had definitely come from the door in front of her. Leah didn't give herself time to hesitate and pushed on that door too. She was outside the main bedroom. A large double bed was fixed to a large grey padded headboard and there were spectacles perched on a Kindle on the cupboard beside it.

The bed was empty and neatly made, two corners drawn back ready for the couple to climb in. Leah surveyed the rest of the room. There were two large wall-to-ceiling doors on runners to her left.

The cat meowed again mournfully

Leah identified where it was coming from. There was a door to the right of the bed. Looked like the en suite. That was why there was an echo. She crossed the terracotta rug in front of the bed and stopped outside the door. It was open about half a foot.

'What are you doing in there?' But she couldn't misdirect herself with the idea that she was only searching for the cat.

The animal was silent but she heard a squeaking sound.

Leah put her fingertips against the panel, and it gave easily. One slight nudge would open it wide.

The noise came again. Like a wet finger running down a polished surface.

'Puss, puss.' She exerted pressure on the door, put all her fingers against it and shoved.

Find the cat.

The animal was looking at her and made a guttural sound as it was revealed.

Leah's hand went to her mouth as she saw what was wrong with it.

Chapter Forty-Three

Two and a half hours earlier

Tate parked his silver Nissan in the small car park for the bowling green again and entered Minster Street the way he had the previous night, avoiding the cameras. He walked on the side of the road opposite Leah's house. He didn't look across to it and tried to appear as casual as possible. He passed two occupied cars but resisted the temptation to peer directly into them. Even though he'd just driven from Eddington Park and made a note of the officers who had watched for his surrender at the gates, he guessed they might have posted at least one here.

He didn't cross the road until he came to the right turn he'd used to access the rear of the properties. Would there be officers positioned there now? If there were any present, he'd just keep on walking.

There wasn't a sign of anyone in the street, however, so

he slipped down the lane and picked his way through the brambles.

When he reached Leah's slightly open gate he crept past it to the next one. Would her neighbours be in? He hadn't dared look up their driveway to see if there was a car there. Not if there were police watching. But before he could touch the panel of the gate, he could hear activity from the other side. Metal over gravel. He stood stock still as the methodical sound got closer. He looked up and down the pathway. Nobody coming either way. If the neighbour came out, he had the privacy to deal with them.

A few moments later he could hear an approaching set of footsteps over the sound, which abruptly stopped.

'Thanks,' a male voice said then slurped from a cup.

'Why don't you use the leaf hoover?'

'Sucks up too much of the gravel. The rake's better,' the male neighbour replied brusquely.

Tate hadn't been able to get a good look at them through the window last night, but they sounded elderly.

'You're not playing for time down here because the log burner needs cleaning?'

'I told you, I'll get to it,' he snapped.

'Less of the tone.'

'You've asked me six times this morning and I said I'll get to it.'

There was a pause as the male neighbour slurped from his cup again.

Tate moved closer to the mossy green panel of the gate and calculated he was about three feet from the couple. He put his fingers on the handle.

'She's still not back next door,' the female neighbour reported.

The raking started then halted. 'You going round there when she is?'

'Just to make sure she's OK,' she assured him. 'Must be serious if the police are involved.'

Tate could hear a scratching as the male neighbour thoughtfully stroked his beard bristles.

'I knew things were getting worse between her and Elliot,' she continued.

'How?'

'Heard them arguing when they had the kitchen window open last week. That's what not having children does to you.'

The male neighbour sighed. 'It's none of our business.' He dragged the rake across the gravel a couple of times then stopped again. 'I'm sure I've seen that girl that dropped Elliot off before. Maybe she worked in The Black Horse at one time.'

'Got a good memory for that sort of thing, haven't you?' He carried on raking. Didn't reply.

'What about her man who sneaked out last night?' the female neighbour pushed.

Tate stiffened. They *had* watched him leave.

The male neighbour stopped raking again. 'Not seen him before.'

'Very embarrassing. Their secret flames almost passed each other in the driveway.'

'Maybe they're not a secret,' the male neighbour speculated.

'Elliot definitely didn't want that girl hanging around. You saw that.' There was a trace of glee in her voice.

'It's none of our business,' he repeated and started raking again.

'I'll speak to her when she comes home.'

'Doesn't look like Elliot will be. He had a bag with him when he left.'

'Perhaps she's thrown him out,' she wondered, breathlessly.

But Tate knew where Elliot was. Exactly where he'd left him.

'Still don't know why the police would have turned up like that though.' Her feet crunched as she started to head back to the house.

Should he put them out of their misery? Tate tried the handle, but the gate was stuck. He booted the wood hard and it opened with the second impact.

He jerked the rake out of the old man's hand. Two hard swipes and the couple were cowering bloodied on the floor. 'Get up.'

They struggled shakily to their feet and she held up her hands as if he were holding a gun.

'Walk inside and lead me to the bathroom.'

Chapter Forty-Four

The ginger cat was trying to get out of the far end of the deep bath nearest the taps, its paws skating and squeaking on the buttermilk acrylic. But Leah saw the Trents first. They were face down on top of each other in the bath, four feet hooked over the end nearest her – one with a backless pink slipper hanging from it.

Her brain reluctantly absorbed the details of what was in front of her. There was no water in the bath but the cat's escape was being frustrated by the dark rivulets that spattered the sides. The blood was sprayed over the gold-yellow wall tiles, streaks that had trickled back down and set in thick lines on the grouting and along the shelf.

The animal's paws paddled against the stained bath, its claws making a frantic clicking as the muscles rippled under its dyed fur.

Leah couldn't move. Somewhere between her instinct to rescue the cat and the repellent spectacle before her cancelled out any ability to react.

The animal groaned as it tried again.

'Mr and Mrs Trent?' It seemed as if Leah's voice was coming from somewhere behind her.

Their bodies were quite motionless.

Leah's attention was drawn from the trapped cat to the powder-blue bathmat. There was a maroon pool there and something in it glinted the illuminated overhead strip bulb. There were three razor blades submerged in the thick liquid.

The cat finally got free and managed to clamber awkwardly onto the taps before turning its body and glaring at Leah. It hissed as it hunched low.

She'd only been talking to them a few hours previously. All she could smell was a potent, antiseptic pine aroma.

The cat thudded onto the floor as it left its perch, its paws submerged in the blood on the bathmat. It bent its head to sniff what it was standing in.

'Mr and Mrs Trent?' She had to make sure of what she already knew.

The cat shot out of the bathroom, jinking around her legs but Leah stayed rooted to the spot. She could see their clothes were wet. Had he drowned them in the bath and then pulled the plug? Cut their throats?

When I work, I prefer not to have any interruptions.

Had he needed three razor blades? Leah's eyes were drawn back to them, set in the congealing puddle. She took a step towards the bath and saw her arm extend and retract. She had to touch a part of their bodies. They could still be alive.

Her hand was out again, fingers moving closer as she

took another three paces to the bath. Now she was looking down into it and gagged as she took in the heads and shoulders of the Trents. Mr Trent was on top of his wife, the back of his bald pate glistening red. Below it she could see the membrane of blood over the hairs in the plughole.

What part of them could she shake? She ran her eyes down their stacked bodies, saw Mrs Trent's hand curled at an unnatural angle under the weight of her husband. Mr Trent's back didn't rise and fall. She couldn't look at them anymore. But she had to check. The only parts of them that weren't saturated with blood were their legs.

She reached out to Mrs Trent's exposed foot. Leah breathed harshly in and then gripped her ankle. It was cold, solid and immovable. She couldn't shake it. She pinched it instead and then retreated when there was no response.

Tate had murdered the elderly couple and then mutilated them with the razor blades while the police watched the house next door.

Leah realised she was standing on the blades and recoiled in horror. Now there were only two there. She wiped her boot on the mat and the third blade came unstuck.

She headed back into the bedroom and pulled the door closed hard behind her. She leaned back on the panel and looked down at the smeared bloody footprints she'd left on the tan carpet. A set of red pawprints stretched from her to the bed. The cat was curled up at the white pillows, dark smears all over them. It watched her impassively, its green eyes not comprehending the fear in hers.

All she could hear was the animal's harsh breath as its chest pumped in and out.

Her phone vibrated in her back pocket and it felt like an electric shock.

'The police are outside.' Tate said as soon as she'd answered.

Leah tried to respond but only a choked noise escaped her.

'Are you in the bedroom?'

'Yes.'

'Go over to the window then. You'll see them parked in the road.'

Was he watching her? Leah lifted herself away from the door and crossed the carpet to the horizontal blinds at the pane. Her fingers fumbled them open. She could see over the hedge and all the way up the street. There were two cars on the opposite side of the road with people sitting in the driver's seat. 'How could you have...' Repugnance bulged out of the unfinished question.

'You're enquiring about my method?'

'They were strangers to you.'

'And that doesn't make them easier targets?'

'They were defenceless...'

'See my last answer.'

Leah blinked away a tear.

'You seem to be having more trouble dealing with this than you did Katya. Is that because you didn't know her?'

She gagged again.

'Or because she'd been sleeping with Elliot? I didn't

know the old couple. That's why it was easy. Were they really good neighbours?' But he sounded bored.

Leah felt cold nausea trickle through her.

'Take a breath. You need to compose yourself for someone you really care about.'

Chapter Forty-Five

'**M**rs Talbot?' DI Byrne had taken the phone from Fitch.

'Yes. Can I pick up my car?' Leah was striding shakily back down the rear path, brambles snagging her legs.

'Are you OK?'

'Fine. I just wanted to check with you it's all right. I need it now.'

'Are you not at your father's place?' Byrne sounded puzzled.

Leah remembered she'd told the officer she was on her way there when she'd left the police station. And that had been some time ago. 'No.' She tried to slow her breathing down. 'I ... had some other things to sort out first. Who's got my keys?'

'The attending officer will have them. I'll call ahead and let him know you're going to pick the vehicle up.'

'Thanks. I won't disturb you any longer.'

'Just so you know, we've released Lownes.'

Momentarily Leah had forgotten who he was.

'There seemed little point in holding him further.'

'OK, thanks.'

'Where are you now?'

Leah had been about to hang up. Now she had to think on her feet. She couldn't tell her she was in Minster Street. 'Just on my way to Alice Booth's house.'

There was a pause. 'Uh-huh.'

Leah wondered if her non-specific answer had made Byrne suspicious. 'Should be there in five minutes.'

'And *then* you're going to your father's house?'

'Yes. Will you be in touch if there's any news?' she added, trying to act like she should.

'I've already said we will,' Byrne said flatly. 'Are you sure you're OK?'

'Yes. Everything's fine.' Which was a stupid thing to say.

'OK.' Byrne conceded uncertainly. 'Keep your phone with you.'

'Of course.' She heard Byrne hang up. The officer was clearly sceptical but Leah didn't have time to worry about it. She had to get the car and drive to the location that Tate had just given her.

Ten minutes later she was walking back along the grass bank to the home of Alice Booth. She was still numb from her horrific experience in the Trents's bathroom. Her fingerprints had to be at Katya's place as well as her neighbours' house. Was Tate deliberately incriminating her?

And was he nearby, observing her every move? If he was, she wouldn't linger long at Alice Booth's. She needed the car but she had to avoid him thinking she was communicating with the police. If they detained her with more questions what would happen to Elliot?

She tried to examine the face of each motorist that passed her on the road, and shot wary glances behind her. No sign of Tate. But she couldn't afford to assume he wasn't around. Only she could resolve the situation, so she had to shut away the sickening images in her head and focus on what she had to do.

There were only three cars parked outside now, two patrol vehicles and Elliot's Vauxhall. The gate was open, but Leah remained outside the property. The same older uniformed officer was standing in the courtyard talking on his mobile. He hung up as soon as he saw Leah and ambled over.

'DI Byrne said she was phoning ahead.'

He nodded, his fingers already in his pocket for the keys. He handed them to her.

'Thanks.'

The officer didn't respond, just studied Leah.

She lingered, expecting him to say something else but he didn't.

As she made for the car, she could feel his eyes on her back. After their conversation, had Byrne told him to watch her? Suddenly the distance between her and the Vauxhall seemed far greater than it was, and she tried to slow her pace down. Leah didn't look back but got in and pulled the door closed behind her. She tried to start the engine, but it wouldn't. Glancing at her mirror she saw the officer still at the gate, his attention fixed on her car. 'Come on.'

The Vauxhall turned over, sputtered and cut out.

Leah attempted to remain composed and tried again.

The car still wouldn't start.

Was this a ruse by Byrne? Did they still have suspicions about her and want to keep the vehicle? Surely they could have fingerprinted it by now if they'd wanted to. But perhaps they wanted to do other tests on it and this was their way—

It started up the fourth time.

Leah puffed out a breath of relief and pulled out onto the road as soon as there was a gap in the traffic. She U-turned, accelerated away and checked her mirror. The officer still hadn't budged. Was he going to report back to Byrne now?

As Leah put her foot down, the officer disappeared behind the curve of the road. She couldn't allow the police to follow her. She peered at the other vehicles behind her. Were any of them surveillance officers that Byrne had dispatched from their vigil outside her house?

She realised the deer had been removed. No sign of the carcass she'd left there remained. Had Alice Booth also been taken away? If she had there were still three other dead people behind her in Forley, and the police were still to discover them. Was she really capable of withholding that? The knowledge of it burnt at her. She would tell DI Byrne as soon as possible but she had to do everything in her power to save Elliot's life first.

Leah grimly gripped the steering wheel and tried not to

imagine what was happening to Elliot at that very moment. At least she now knew where he was being held. That's if Tate wasn't lying to her. Maybe he was sending her there as part of a game.

She slowed down at the bend. If she wasn't careful, she'd crash the car before she got there.

Stay calm. Just follow instructions.

If Tate genuinely wanted her, if his feelings for her really weren't another lie, she could use them to get Elliot back. It was the only leverage she had. She knew there was a mini toolkit in the back. Underneath the spare wheel. Leah was sure there was a crowbar in there she could use as a weapon. There was no time to arm herself with anything else. He'd said half an hour.

Her watch told her it had already been fifteen minutes since she'd left the Trents's house after he'd told her where to meet him.

The sign came into view. Even though it was just outside Forley, she'd only ever used the front of the property to turn her car around on a handful of occasions. She stopped in the middle of the road. The cars behind her passed by. Would any of them be watching in their rear mirrors for where she was going? She couldn't hesitate.

Leah tried to swallow her fear as she turned right and headed over the gravelled area, her tyres popping as she drove straight through the rusted and now open gates of the old pig farm.

Chapter Forty-Six

Tate's instructions on the phone had been clear. *Come to Enclosure D. We'll be waiting.*

As she passed through the third open gate, the space opened up and Leah was surprised at just how big the pig farm was. She halted the car at a blue metal sign on a low brick wall and squinted through the rust spots. An arrow pointed right to B–D so she followed it around a curved overgrown track until she came to a large, dilapidated corrugated iron building.

Decelerating she scanned the lichen-coated metal façade and spotted a faded yellow B above the double sliding doors at the front. She shifted off again, the track getting progressively more overgrown as she passed C and then came to the last corrugated structure, slumped and skulking under the soiled silver clouds.

It was the largest one and the sliding door was open, a square of solid darkness awaiting her arrival. Leah turned off the engine and registered how quiet it was. She couldn't even hear the traffic on Plough Lane and she remained in her seat, scrutinising the enclosure and its surroundings. Behind it she could see a barbed-wire boundary fence, ragged plastic and rubbish clinging to the top. Tate had brought her to the furthest outbuilding from the road.

Rain started pattering lightly on the roof of the car.

The farm had clearly been abandoned for some time. It had certainly been closed as long as she and Elliot had lived in Forley and it was definitely a place where Tate wouldn't have any interruptions.

Leah wondered: if she walked in there, would she ever walk out again? But she had to go inside. The longer she hesitated, the harder it would be. She balled her insides in readiness and heaved herself out of the car. She closed the door and the harsh sound bounced off the building. Was he watching her now?

She went to the rear of the car and found the rolled-up leather toolkit. The mini crowbar was the heaviest. Her hand shook as she replaced the rest and shut the door. She locked the car and pocketed the key. It was a long way back to the main gate.

Taking a few steps forward, boots crunching on the damp gravel, she tried to prevent her frame trembling by gripping the crowbar harder. She slowed and stopped. Her attention was on the black space before her. She couldn't go in there. It had to be a trap. Was Elliot even still alive? She'd been batting away that thought since their phone conversation but now she had to consider the implications. With the Trents dead, Leah might be the only one left who'd seen Tate's face. If she entered, she would surely be making his job easy.

But she had to keep reminding herself that Tate could have disposed of her when she'd been unconscious in Alice Booth's home. Maybe he'd changed his mind now though. Perhaps he'd realised she was too much of a liability and had to be quickly dealt with. Why else lure her here?

She couldn't physically put another foot forward. The silent blackness before her looked impenetrable. There was no glimpse of anything beyond it. 'I'm here,' she declared and it was loud enough to echo back from the interior.

No reply from within.

'Where's Elliot?' Her right leg quivered, and she readjusted her footing.

Silence.

He was somewhere near, waiting for her to go inside. Would the door slam on her? Would she find Elliot in the same state as the Trents and would he then kill her and take his time afterwards? 'I'm not coming inside until I see him.' She shot a glance behind, expecting Tate to be stealing up on her.

She turned quickly to the front again and waited. The wind blew suddenly hard at her right side and she twisted her head so her ear wasn't blocked by the blast. He wasn't going to respond. He'd told her where she had to go.

It felt like a significant exertion to move herself forward but she managed to cover another few feet. It took her close enough to the building to hear liquid dripping rhythmically inside.

But now she could make out some shapes ahead. The

low rails of the pig pens and the long feed troughs below. Leah kept moving steadily forward, her ears straining for other sounds.

She reached the doors and peered left and right. Nobody was lurking either side of the runners in the floor. A chain and padlock lay just inside. Even though the place had been empty for so long, a mixture of ingrained and sour smells prickled her nose – swine and feed and urine. She fought back a cough, let her eyes get used to the gloom. The pens stretched away as far as she could see. It would have been deafening inside when it was full of livestock. 'What now?' She raised her voice.

Its resonation chilled her, the two words ricocheting off the walls. She still hadn't stepped inside. But he knew she would. Leah guessed he wouldn't speak until she had. She brandished the mini crowbar but the cold metal in her palm didn't make her feel any less vulnerable.

She took two paces forward and the atmosphere settled on her, the aroma suddenly cloying. She could see further inside but not as far as the back wall. She took out her phone and turned on the torch. There was a wide concrete walkway ahead that bisected the pens either side. Leah headed tentatively down it, her footfalls fed back to her as she shone the beam into each pen she passed.

Half a minute later the torch caught the edge of a sign above.

DISPATCH AND PROCESSING. BOOTS AND OVERALLS TO BE WORN AT ALL TIMES.

Her skin tightened on her scalp as she realised she was walking into an abattoir. Leah was a vegetarian and hadn't eaten meat since the turn of the century. This was the sort of vile place she'd only seen in documentaries. How many thousands of animals had passed through here, prodded and poked towards an undignified production-line fate?

Leah halted and shone the torch up ahead. It highlighted a corrugated wall with a smaller doorway. Thick, faded blue strips of plastic hung down in place of a door. Goods in and out but enough of a barrier to keep the flies away.

A low tapping noise came from behind her.

Leah whirled around, crowbar and torch held up. The beam caught a small furry body as it darted out of sight, her glimpse of its link tail confirming what it was. She restrained the revulsion she would normally have felt. Had the rat been the only source of the sound? She could see the daylight through the doorway behind her, but it seemed so far away now.

She quickly returned the light to the entrance up ahead. 'You've got me inside. Speak to me.'

He didn't.

Leah had to walk through the drapes. As soon as she did, she'd be away from the daylight. But even if he'd attacked her at the car, nobody would have heard. She was alone with no choice.

Leah could hear the circulation pumping through her whole frame as she continued ahead and put her hand on the cold plastic.

Chapter Forty-Seven

L eah passed through the drapes, her arm extended as she shone her torch ahead. There was a different aroma in here. A richer but gamier smell. She had to be near the back of the structure by now. The beam picked up the edge of what she initially thought was a table but as she played the light over it, she could see it was a large circular conveyor belt.

The torch caught some shapes above and as Leah illuminated them, she realised they were rows of hooks. This was definitely where the animals used to be slaughtered. She tilted the phone down and could see the large open drain-hole at the centre of a metallic basin.

The drapes closed behind her and she darted the beam around the corrugated walls. Any moment she expected it to pick out a face. His face. But as she breathed erratically with each movement of the light, she couldn't see any sign of him or Elliot.

Beyond a large rusted white gas cylinder which was

connected to a hose gun on a stand she could discern two aluminium doors. They were part of a small box structure to the right of the space. Leah stood still for a moment and listened.

The only noise was a low wind blowing through the gaps in the roof and the rain rattling behind it.

She clutched the crowbar. 'Are you in here?'

Something scuttled to her right, but her torch wasn't fast enough to pinpoint it. She started walking towards the doors, swinging the beam from side to side and up to the steel joists above until she was standing at the bottom of three metallic steps that led up to a platform.

The steps complained as she put her weight onto them, and the platform wobbled slightly when she was standing between the two doors. They both had identical rusted steel handles.

She had to open them. That was the reason he'd directed her in here. Was he waiting behind one? She strained her ears for sounds of breathing. Nothing. That scared her even more. What if Elliot was here, left to suffocate? She was wasting time.

She chose the left door in front of her, raised the crowbar and tugged the handle with her other. She aimed the light inside.

It was a refrigeration room, more hooks dangling from rails. There was debris on the floor – beer cans and cigarette ends. She could also make out some used syringes there as well. How old were they and had Tate subdued Elliot by injecting him?

She turned around suddenly, expecting somebody to be

preparing to push her inside but there was no movement and only the noise of her feet settling on the platform.

Leah began to feel that she was alone. And the notion that the next room was empty too seemed more terrifying than finding Tate in it. Was he just stringing her along, enjoying her torment? She tugged the second door, bracing herself for what she'd find.

The torch hit the blank rust-spotted back wall with its identical rails and hooks. She flitted it around the floor. More leftovers from a junkie party.

There was a dark shape there though. To the right and towards the rear. Leah's beam halted on it. She ran it down its length and could make out the dirty soles of a pair of trainers. The light trembled as she tried to hold it steady. 'Who is that?'

The shape didn't budge.

A low rumble built in Leah's head. She recognised the waterproof light-blue jacket. It was the hooded one Elliot had been wearing when he'd left for the station that morning. 'Elliot?' She said, louder, her voice cracking.

Still no response.

Leah moved inside the room, her hand holding open the panel. 'Elliot?' She'd said it loudly enough. He should have heard. Maybe he was sedated.

Despite her frantic need to reach Elliot she spun round again, the torch going in every direction but finding nobody. She returned her attention to the motionless figure. As she took another pace forward, she could see that he was facing the wall.

The rumble became a boom, the pressure building to the

moment she'd been dreading since she first had the phone call from Tate. He'd shown no mercy to Alice Booth, Katya Boyers or the Trents. Why would he towards a man he saw as a threat?

She covered the space between the door and where he was lying, but now she didn't want to touch him. Leah tried to hold the beam steady. He was quite still. 'Elliot?'

The door closed gently behind her, but she scarcely registered it.

She leaned over him. The hood was up and covering the side of his face. She whispered his name now, waited for any tiny movement. She couldn't contemplate the reason for him being so still.

Leah put the crowbar under her left armpit, reached out and put her right hand on his shoulder. He didn't flinch. The flesh was solid in her fingers. She gripped it harder, parted her feet and tensed her stomach. She tried to turn him, attempted to roll him towards her like she had Katya. He was too heavy.

Leah recalled the Trents in the bath. Their dead weight face down in their drained blood.

The body came with her third tug, twisting around, the back of his hand slapping against the floor.

Leah could see the blood on the side of the light-blue hood. One half of his face had been in a dark pool. It had been scored, multiple times. Slits cut at all angles in his cheeks, through his eyes and across his chin. But Leah still recognised him.

She straightened, her torch still spotlighting the notched features, her arm trembling as she took them in and a gasp escaped her. Her brain grappled with the dead expression before she realised how recently she'd seen it. It was Lownes, the man who had approached DI Byrne at the park gates.

As she repositioned her feet, her left boot slid in the dark slick that had been discharged by the movement of his body. Her low sound of revulsion seemed amplified by the low ceiling. There was a deep gash across his throat. He was quite dead. When had Byrne said he'd been released from custody?

Her beam remained on his face, his dead stare and his slit eyelids. Not looking away as if reassuring herself that it wasn't Elliot. But Tate had dressed him in Elliot's coat. Murdering an innocent man to deliberately traumatise her into believing it was her husband.

She remained there for another few seconds before lowering the light. But the image of his shredded face remained burnt into her vision as she turned and stumbled back to the door.

Using both hands she wrenched down hard on the handle.

It clicked and the door swung out.

Chapter Forty-Eight

L eah had to get out of the enclosure. Lownes and his mutilated face were behind her now, but every detail was settling in her mind. She was desperate to breathe fresh air. The darkness and the aroma had inflated a balloon in her chest that felt like it was about to burst.

Gripping the mini crowbar, she staggered down the steps. Leah swung her torch from side to side and headed for the plastic drapes.

Passing through them to the walkway, she anticipated footfalls behind her. Was Lownes the only reason Tate had summoned her to this place, dressing him in Elliot's jacket to illustrate just what he was prepared to do if she wasn't obedient? Or was he still concealed somewhere nearby? And what had he done with Elliot?

But she had to get out before the horror of the place overcame her. She started to run, the beam bouncing before her as she pumped her arms. The square of dirty white light at the doors grew bigger as she allowed herself to suck in a breath. If he was here, would he really let her leave?

She was about twenty feet from the sliding doors when she heard the noise. She slowed, whipping the torch behind her and confirming there was nobody there before she returned her attention to the entrance.

A car was pulling up outside.

Leah darted left and moved more slowly towards the door, using its edge as cover. Lurking in the shadows, she squinted against the daylight. It was a purple car and it had just finished parking next to hers.

As the door opened, she reversed a couple of steps. A pot-bellied, bearded man in a dark leather jacket emerged and quickly assessed his surroundings before quietly clicking his door shut. Leah shone the beam behind her again; the walkway was still empty.

In front of her, the man was looking over her car. He peered through the driver's window and then took in the building.

Leah retreated another pace. Was he a police officer who had followed her from Alice Booth's place?

As if to answer her question, the man took out a radio from his inside jacket pocket and spoke into it. 'Just driven to the last enclosure. D. Her car's parked outside.'

There was a response from the radio that Leah couldn't hear.

'The door is open so am assuming she's inside.'

Another incoherent reply.

'OK. Will hold fire until you arrive.' The man put away his radio but started strolling towards the building.

Leah fought the impulse to approach him. She reminded herself that, if she did, she might never see Elliot again.

The man hesitated as he reached the doors, his expression nervous.

Leah slunk away, pointing her light at the floor and finding the rail of the pen. She could run her hand along it and use it as a guide. She swiped off the torch and looked back.

The police officer's figure appeared at the door, but he seemed reluctant to enter.

Leah crouched where she was and didn't make a sound.

The police officer stepped over the threshold and the beam of his phone torch came on.

It was too weak to reach Leah where she was, but she slid further along the pen, so she was in the deep shadows.

The police officer remained in his position.

She couldn't afford to give her location away and prayed she didn't disturb anything on the ground as she followed the pen to its far edge. If he found her, she'd have to tell him exactly what she was doing here. Was there another way out of the enclosure? She let go of the rail. Extending her hands, she carefully shuffled forward until her palms connected with cold, damp corrugated metal. She was at the wall. Maybe there was a side door. Chances were, it was going to be locked though.

Her phone rang.

Leah quickly scrabbled it out of her pocket and silenced it after two rings.

'Who's that? Mrs Talbot?'

Leah put a hand over her mouth, as if she didn't trust herself to stay quiet.

'Mrs Talbot, are you all right?'

She clenched her palm tight to her lips.

'I'm Police Constable Miles. Are you OK?' His voice echoed around the space.

Leah watched him take three steps inside and swing his light around. She crouched until her knee touched the floor.

'Do you need help?'

When she still didn't reply, Leah watched his outline stiffen.

'OK. Backup's on the way. If you can hear me, walk to the front of the building.' He tried to sound officious but there was tension in his voice.

She stayed put and watched him venture further in, his torch now pointed between the pens.

The police officer paused. 'If you can hear me, walk towards my voice.' He waited.

Leah guessed he was hoping he didn't have to go any further.

After a few moments of realising he did, the police officer started making his way down the walkway.

Leah held her breath as his beam moved into her line of sight and then went beyond it. Should she risk trying to leave via the front entrance or would he see her silhouetted there and quickly intercept her?

'Mrs Talbot?' He briefly shone his phone back behind him before returning it to the path Leah had just followed.

He was now halfway along the walkway. Soon he'd be entering the dispatch area where Lownes was. Leah stood upright and crept towards the entrance. If she stayed in the shadows she could sidle right up to the door and only be visible when she slipped around the edge.

'Mrs Talbot?' He was at the drapes now.

Leah didn't wait to find out if he was brave enough to enter. She strode towards the door, clenching herself as the daylight eventually fell on her face.

Chapter Forty-Nine

When Leah got outside, she swivelled back and saw the officer's torch beam playing over the drapes. Looked like he was in two minds about whether to enter. In minutes he'd find Lownes, and she had to be long gone by then.

She walked delicately over the gravel towards her car. If she started the engine, he would definitely hear her. How long would it take him to exit the building? Time enough for her to get off the site, or would he be able to catch up to her in his car? It sounded like his colleagues were about to arrive. If she went on foot, she could skirt the enclosures and stay out of sight of police vehicles coming the other way.

Was she meant to stay on the pig farm? She quickly checked her phone. It was a missed call from her father.

Leah looked back again. Had she missed something else in there? Something the officer was about to find? Surely if Tate had been lying in wait, he would have made himself known to her before she'd left. Maybe he was giving her time to find the body before he called her with his next instructions. Being in the daylight did nothing to shift the spectre of Lownes and his carved-up face. She had to get away from the officer. Couldn't afford to have him delay her and start asking questions while Elliot was still a prisoner.

Leah cringed as she used her fob to unlock the car doors but then a thought struck her. She peered in through the officer's window and spotted his keys still in the ignition. She painstakingly opened his door, slid them out and then pocketed them. She'd hand them back when this was all over.

She got in her own car and threw the crowbar in the back. Once she started the engine, she'd have to shoot out of there as fast as she could. There was plenty of room in front of the enclosure though so Leah calculated she could easily exit in one arc and not have to slow down. She took a breath.

Suddenly there was the buzz of an approaching engine.

Leah froze and listened. It was definitely coming towards her. Must be the backup the officer had mentioned. Should she go regardless? The track in had been tight. They could easily block her escape.

She swiftly got out of the car. Scrambling behind it to the bushes there, she skirted the edge until she came to the side of the road leading in. Leah pressed herself to a fence post.

The engine got louder and a few moments later a yellow car entered the area in front of the outbuilding. As soon as it had passed, she slipped around the corner and scrambled up the track until she'd rounded the bend. Had they spotted her in the rear-view?

Leah waited there, chest heaving. She heard the engine switch off and two doors slam. Footsteps over gravel. Were they heading up the track towards her? The footfalls didn't get louder. They changed pitch. They were following the first officer inside the enclosure.

She turned and started jogging along the track. She would get off it as soon as she could; just in case there were more cars headed the same way. Get behind the next enclosure, stay out of sight and decide what to do next.

Leah's phone buzzed in her hand.

DAD.

She didn't have time. But what if he'd had another fall in the shower? She would answer him quickly, find out if he was OK and tell him she'd call back.

'Olivia?'

'No, Dad. It's Leah.'

'Yes,' he dismissed, grouchily. 'Is your mother with you?'

Leah briefly closed her eyes. There was no time for the usual conversation. 'No, she's not.'

'Well, she's not here.' There was accusation in his voice.

'I'm in the middle of something, Dad. I'll call you back as soon as I can.'

'I need to go outside but I can't find the key to the garage.'

That wasn't good. The last time he'd journeyed out they'd found him in the local library after hours of searching. Panic heaped on panic. 'There's no need for you to go to the garage.' Leah had the key. It was permanently locked up. They'd had to sell the car to stop him from wanting to take it for a spin, but he often assumed it was still in there. 'You can't go out in the BMW, Dad.'

'I know that,' he said with hostility, as if she were patronising him. 'I just need the key.'

Leah trotted faster down the path. 'What for?'

Silence. He'd forgotten.

'You don't need to go out there. It's freezing today. Stay in the warm and I'll be there as soon as I can.' She felt a pang of guilt, knowing that as soon as he'd put the phone down, the promise would be forgotten anyway.

'Ah, wait. I do remember. I need to get some things out but I'm not sure where they are. Put your mother on.'

'She's not here.' Leah could feel her chest tightening. 'Don't try to go out there. Promise me. I have to hang up now.'

'Don't know why I bothered calling. I'll find them myself.'

Leah stopped on the track. 'There's nothing out there you need, Dad.'

'How do you know?' he snapped.

'The car is gone, Mum's gone – she died two years ago, and you were too ill to go to the funeral!'

Silence.

Leah sighed. It wasn't the first time she'd broken the news to him but never with such anger. It would be forgotten but for the following moments it would be as raw to him as the first time she'd told him. 'Dad...'

'I remember that. I know…' But his voice was small, his confusion barely concealed.

She steadied her voice. 'I'll be coming as soon as I can. Just see what's on TV 'til I get there.'

He sniffed. 'Now you've got me upset in front of my guest.'

Leah started to shake her head but froze. 'What guest?'

'Your friend. The one who wants the things from the garage.'

'What friend, Dad?' The booming in her head was back.

The phone clunked. A low voice spoke to her father.

Leah immediately recognised it.

He breathed in before he addressed her. 'Now this is the sort of place that I can really inhabit. Care to join us?'

Chapter Fifty

Leah's stomach lurched and Tate's presence in her father's world struck her briefly dumb.

'Did you find Lownes?'

'What are you doing *there*?'

'I needed somewhere intimate. This cottage is really something. Chocolate box.'

'Don't you dare hurt him.' How had he inveigled his way in?

'Why don't you rustle up that coffee you were talking about?' Tate said away from the phone.

Leah heard her father say something incoherent and his footsteps shuffle off to the kitchen. 'Get out of there. Now.' She couldn't restrain her anger.

'But we've made ourselves at home.'

'We?'

'Elliot and I.'

Should she be relieved or was he lying? 'Put Elliot on.'

'Unable to. He's still in the car.'

Leah imagined him tied up there. If he was there at all. 'I'm not doing anything until I speak to Elliot and you get out of that house.'

'The kettle's on again. It would be rude of me to refuse your father's hospitality.'

'Why have you involved him?' But she already knew the answer.

'Making sure you know what's at stake. With all Elliot's done I wouldn't blame you for leaving him in my tender care but your father ... he seems like a good man.'

Hatred coursed through Leah now. 'He's got Alzheimer's.'

'Yes, Elliot told me. Pretty advanced too. I've told your father I'm Elliot. I could see he doubted that when he opened the door and I introduced myself. But I think he's playing along because he's not sure.'

'I'll meet you anywhere. Do anything you ask.'

'You've promised that already.'

'And I've done it!'

'Sorry. Do you have sugar? I should know by now...' her father said from the kitchen.

'No sugar for me.'

'What did you want from the garage?' Leah demanded.

'Said I needed to borrow his tools.' Tate lowered his voice. 'He's been very helpful, but he can't find the key.'

'I have the key. It's in the drawer at home.'

'Not much use there then. I'll have to improvise with what I can find in the house.'

'Tell me where you want to meet me.' Her plea dried in her throat.

'I think here's good. We have privacy. Oh, thank you.'

Leah could visualise Tate accepting a cup from her father.

'Go and take the weight off and we can have a good catch-up.' Tate said to him. A few seconds' pause. 'Anything I should know, to put him at his ease while we wait for you to arrive?'

'I told the police I was going to visit him,' she blurted.

A moment's silence. 'Why would you tell them that?' he asked sceptically. 'You were going to the pig farm like Mr Lownes. I told him he could have the rest of his money when he met me there. I don't think he could have been trusted to spend it wisely though.'

Leah repelled the image of his mutilated face. 'Before I left the police station, I told them I was going to the cottage. They took the address from me.'

'That's very convenient.' But there was doubt in his voice.

'I always visit him on Saturday afternoon.'

'Maybe I should ask him.'

'You can ... but he may not remember.' She could already hear Tate's footsteps moving across the lounge floor.

'Expecting you daughter today?'

'Olivia? Yes,' her father responded confidently.

'That's my sister. He often thinks I'm her. I visit every Saturday. That's why I gave the police the address. You'd better get out of there. They're here at the farm. They must have followed me. I lost them but if they can't find me here...'

'Then you'd obviously go to the place you gave them the address for.' Tate replied sardonically.

'They'd have to check it.'

'You're right.' But Tate didn't seem perturbed.

'What's going on? Is Olivia not coming?'

'Everything's fine,' Tate placated her father.

'Ask her about the garage key.'

'She says it's at home.' Tate informed him.

'Well, it's not much good there, is it?'

'I have to agree with your dad.'

Leah thought fast. 'There's a fishing lake, not ten minutes from where you are. In the grounds of a stately home. Isherwood Manor. It's been closed down, but you can still access the lake behind the house. Nobody goes there.'

'But *we* could?'

'Yes. I can be there in twenty minutes.'

'No,' he eventually replied. 'I have everything I need here. I'll keep your father company until you arrive.'

Tate hung up.

Chapter Fifty-One

Leah tried twice to call him back, but her father's phone was engaged. She got nothing but the answering service when she rang Elliot's number. She remained motionless on the track, staring at the screen. She was paralysed, unable to decide what to do next. She had to get away from the farm and the police. God knows how long a cab would take to reach her. She turned the way she'd come. They were bound to have found Lownes by now. Would that keep them occupied?

She hurried back to the enclosure and slowed her pace as she reached the entrance by the bushes. She couldn't hear any voices. Leah stole into the gravelled parking area. Three cars in a row now but nobody in evidence.

Should she risk it? If they caught up with her, she would be in a worse position than she was now. She couldn't jeopardise her father and Elliot's lives by telling them about Tate being at the cottage and it was likely they'd hold her because of the body they'd just discovered.

Getting her car was still the best option. She listened and could just make out low conversation from inside the building. *Go now before it's too late.*

She crept over the gravel, her attention on the open sliding door. No sign of any movement within. Only one car was capable of pursuing her because she had the key to the other. Her eyes shifted to the yellow car that had parked up. She looked in the driver's side. No keys in the ignition. She really had to shift as soon as she started her engine.

Echoing footsteps.

Leah halted and her attention swung back to the enclosure.

The footfalls sped up. At least one person was about to walk out.

Leah trotted to her car, opened it and slid into the seat. She closed the door as quietly as she could and then glanced up at the entrance. Nobody had appeared yet. She fired up the engine.

Two plain-clothes officers emerged from the sliding door. Looked like the ones who had just arrived.

Leah pulled out. She had to drive right at them to turn.

One of them held up his hands.

Leah accelerated hard. 'Out of the way!'

As she closed the gap, the two officers stood their ground.

'Move!' She kept her foot on the pedal. She could see their expressions clearly now. Didn't look like either of them believed she would keep going.

The other waved his arms.

'Go!' She thought of her father and Elliot and prayed they realised she was serious.

The two officers parted and dived in opposite directions. Leah wrenched the wheel and aimed for the exit. The back of the car skewed, and she fought for control. Behind her she could hear shouts and knew they'd be running for their car.

The Vauxhall righted itself and she negotiated the tight exit and was soon bombing back down the track, past the other enclosures towards the rusted sign. She checked her rear-view.

The yellow car appeared about a hundred yards behind her. She was almost at the exit.

The officers' car surged forward and rapidly gained on her.

Leah turned left at the sign and shot to the gates that led to the main road. Please God the traffic wasn't too busy. If she had to pause there for more than a few seconds, they'd catch up to her.

She looked right and left as she rocketed through. A car was coming from her left and she tried to estimate if she had time to pull out in front of it. *No time to think.*

Leah stamped the pedal and dragged the wheel right, turning in front of the oncoming car.

They held their hand down on the horn.

Was there time for them to decelerate?

Leah's head snapped as the car struck her from behind. The impact made the Vauxhall veer to the left. She was hurtling towards a ditch on the edge of the road. She'd lost control.

She jerked the wheel right again but too hard. Now she was careering to the other side.

Leah managed to struggle the car back to the middle before she reached the roadworks there. In her mirror she saw the vehicle that had struck her was slowing down. She hoped they were OK. It had been quite a jolt, but it didn't look like it had been severe enough for their airbag to deploy.

The two officers were close behind and swerved around it before they picked up speed again.

Leah knew there was a roundabout up ahead. But she was approaching the temporary traffic lights for the roadworks and they changed to red before she reached them. Any moment, there would be cars streaming from the opposite direction.

She kept going and willed the Vauxhall to beat the signal for the oncoming traffic. There were only fifty or so yards of roadworks left. Could she make it to the end before the cars blocked her way out?

She darted her eyes to the mirror. The two officers passed the red light as well.

As she rounded the bend of the road Leah could see the traffic. A white van had already surged forward. They would collide with her, unless they saw her and slowed down.

But they kept coming. She was about to be boxed in by it and the police behind and she couldn't allow that to happen. Leah floored it.

She was almost at the end of the roadworks. Could she turn left at the end of them before she hit the van?

The van beeped as she barrelled towards it.

Leah tugged the steering wheel and sharply turned left and the van just grazed her as it passed.

More cars beeped at her as she drove by them, but she'd made it to the roundabout and there were no other vehicles waiting there. She looked back in her mirror and saw the van stopped in front of the officers. They couldn't get through but that wouldn't be the case for long.

Leah joined the roundabout and almost took the second turning for Brockford. But she didn't want them to know she was heading that way so she took the third. There was another route to her father's.

But what would she find when she got there?

Chapter Fifty-Two

As she reached her father's village, Leah wondered if any cameras had photographed her plate. The police would have registered it when they were in pursuit, so it wasn't going to be difficult to find her. But she hadn't spotted any traffic cameras as she'd passed through the little villages of Quigley or Honston. She wished she could take comfort from the fact that the police wouldn't be far behind but if they turned up, it meant she'd be putting her father and Elliot in even more danger.

Regardless of what she did, wouldn't the police send an officer to the place she'd told Byrne she was visiting that day, anyway? Or would it be the last location they'd think she'd go? The only thing she could do was try to get to the cottage as quickly as possible and plead with Tate to release her father and Elliot. That was probably exactly what he wanted but she doubted he planned to let any of them go.

A stark sensation of foreboding overcame her as she drove down the hill to St Mark's Church and took the turning for Menthorn Drive. Hock Cottage came into view through the four bare apple trees at the front. It was a converted cider press that her parents had bought nine years before her mother had died.

She parked outside the single rusted green gate, which was half open. Leah regarded the mini crowbar on the back seat for a moment. She grabbed it, lifted her right jean leg and slid it into her boot on the inside of her shin. Surely he would anticipate her bringing a weapon but she couldn't go in unarmed.

Getting out of the car, her attention was already on the downstairs windows, but she couldn't see any movement. As she walked through the gate, she tried not to limp because of the heavy, cold metal.

She had the key to the front door in her pocket, but hesitated there and pushed the bell, her heart pumping in her wrists.

The door immediately opened, and Tate was standing there, his face as welcoming as it had been when she'd called at Alice Booth's home only the night before.

'Leah Talbot, no problems on the road this time?' The enquiry was convivial.

'Where are they?' she demanded.

'Perhaps you'd better come in first.' He stood back.

What choice did she have?

'Did I bite last time?'

Leah reluctantly stepped over the threshold as naturally as she could. Would he search her as soon as she was inside? She turned and immediately put her back to the old red brick wall in the familiar hallway. She could hear the TV murmuring in the front lounge.

Tate closed the door and swivelled on his heel to her, a look of concern on his face. 'You look very pale. Paler than last night even.'

'Where's my father?'

'Interesting that Elliot's welfare has taken a back seat now.'

'If you've harmed him in any way…'

'Is that because you care for your father more or because you've had time to think about what Elliot has done?'

'Dad!' she yelled without taking her eyes off Tate.

The house was silent except for the TV.

Tate blinked a few times, as if he were also awaiting a response. 'Where's your phone?'

'I turned it off when DI Byrne tried to get hold of me.'

Tate extended his hand.

Leah took it out and gave it to him. He slipped it into his trouser pocket.

'Tell me what you've done with him.'

'He's resting.' Tate's eyes tilted briefly to the ceiling. 'We shouldn't disturb him.'

Was that a trick or was he really up there? Leah fought the reflex to race up the stairs 'I've warned you. The police know I'm coming here.'

'So you said. Were you followed from the farm?'

'They weren't far behind.'

'It's your responsibility to keep them away. If they pull up here, you'll have to do your best.'

'I've just been chased by a police car. They're definitely on their way.'

Tate considered this and nodded.

Leah noted that his trousers no longer had a belt. She could still see it around Katya's throat.

'Sounds like you might have led them here deliberately.'

Leah's face flushed hot. 'I've done everything you've asked of me. Do you think I'd endanger them anymore?'

Tate's eyes darted as he tried to read hers. 'Maybe you're not trying hard enough for Elliot. Maybe, as I said, you care less about what happens to him now.'

Leah opened her mouth to respond but the hall phone rang.

Tate turned in its direction. 'I've only just put it back on the cradle. Does your father get many calls?'

Leah shook her head. 'Dad!'

Tate held up his palm to her. 'Just a moment.' He went to the handset and took it from the base. 'Hello?'

Leah strained to hear the voice the other end. What was he doing?

'Yes. Speaking.'

It was a woman's voice. But Leah still couldn't understand what she was saying.

'My daughter?' His gaze swung to Leah. 'Not today.'

Leah tensed her leg. Could feel the cool metal. How long would it take her to retrieve it? She needed him to turn his back.

'Yes. I'll ask her to call you if I see her. Can you tell me what it's concerning?'

Another incoherent response.

'Wait a minute. I'll write it down. I do forget things very easily, I'm afraid.' But he made no move to the pad beside the phone. 'Police? She's not in trouble, is she? OK, as soon as I see her. So it's DI Byrne.' He repeated and paused as if writing the name and the number that followed down.

Tate's eyes were still on her. He frowned. Could he see what she was concealing?

'I certainly will. Right away.' Tate cut the call and carefully replaced the handset on the base. 'That was to be expected. I don't think they'll be calling in anytime soon though.'

Chapter Fifty-Three

Leah's eyes were on the replaced handset. Had DI Byrne really believed she'd just spoken to her father? There was no reason why not. Unless they knew for sure she was here. She'd lost the police car at the roundabout though. How long would it take them to locate her via cameras? With none in the villages she'd cut through, could they work out where she'd really gone?

'Let's go into the dining room.' He gestured to the door behind him. Then he snatched up the phone handset and put it in his other pocket.

'Elliot brought you here?' How else could Tate have found out about the cottage?

'He didn't really have a choice.'

Leah recalled the three bloodied razor blades she'd stepped on in the Trents's bathroom. 'Where is he?'

'Will you follow me to the dining room?'

Leah didn't move.

Tate raised his hands and walked backwards. 'I'll go first, if you like.'

'Dad! Elliot!' she yelled again.

Tate pushed open the door and entered the room.

It had to be a trap. But if he'd wanted to kill her, he could have already done so. She warily approached the door and looked inside.

Tate was standing at the head of the dining table. Five candles were burning in her mother's old candelabra in the middle and two places were set at either end. There was no sign of her father or Elliot.

'I'm afraid I had to improvise with what I could find. I know you prefer white?' He nodded at the filled crystal glasses.

Leah took in the plate on the mat in front of her.

'Egg mayonnaise. Perfunctory but a classic. Hungry?'

Leah looked sharply up at him.

He caught the disbelief in her eyes. 'I'm starving but I've been waiting for you.'

Leah shook her head. 'Tell me where they are.'

'In good time. I really hope you're not going to dismiss my hospitality a second time. I've gone to a lot of trouble.'

'You expect me to eat ... now?' She couldn't conceal her incredulity.

'You will if you want to see your father or Elliot again,' he stated simply and picked up his wine glass.

Leah shook her head. 'I have to know they're both OK.'

'Of course. But, at the moment, you're giving me no reason to tell you. You're putting me on edge. Sit down.'

Leah didn't move.

'The quicker you indulge me the quicker I indulge you. They're both perfectly safe but only I know where they are. Sit.' He gestured to her high-backed chair and scraped his own out.

She remained standing. 'What do you want?'

'I've just told you.' He sat and nodded towards her chair. 'I would pull it out for you, but I don't want to make you any more nervous.' He took a small sip from his wine glass.

'Not bad. Your father's got good taste.' He unfolded his claret napkin and then regarded her unchanged position. 'I'd have preferred chives, but I could only find rosemary in the garden.'

Leah felt the grotesque situation shift her perception of the table. She looked down at the halved eggs on the plate covered in mayonnaise and sprinkled green. There was a set of cutlery. Was the knife sharp enough to use as a weapon?

He dropped the napkin into his lap. 'No dessert, I'm afraid. Although I don't really do desserts. Couldn't find any cheese either so it's just the two courses.'

Leah grabbed the back of the chair and pulled it out. It felt heavy as she shifted it and slowly sat. The wicker seat creaked as it took her weight.

'I don't want to hear mention of your father or Elliot while we're eating. I want to get to know *you* a bit more. When was the last time anyone wanted to do that?'

'Please.' She looked down at the food in front of her. 'Just let me know they're OK and I'll tell you anything you want to know.'

'I expect you've enjoyed some great family meals around this table.'

She took a breath and realised she had no option but to play along. 'This table was bought by my mother when my parents moved here. I'd left home by then.'

'You see. Wasn't that hard.'

She heard his chair creak and shot her eyes up.

He was leaning across the table, his glass extended. 'Cheers.'

Leah fixed her eyes on him; his expression was expectant. She slowly picked up her glass and slightly extended it.

Tate leaned in further and clinked it. 'To getting to know you, Leah Talbot.' He sat back, seemingly satisfied with progress. 'Right, I am ravenous.' He quickly sipped his wine, put down his glass and picked up his cutlery.

Leah's glass remained in her hand.

'It's not drugged.' He cut a half egg with his knife and popped it in his mouth.

Leah put down the glass.

'Here.' He slid his across the table to her. 'Drink mine if you like. Pass me yours.'

She shook her head. 'I'm not thirsty.'

He sighed, leaned across and switched the glasses. 'I'd like you to have a drink with me.' He chewed on his mouthful and then sprinkled some salt on his egg. He was about to take another morsel but stopped and raised his eyebrows at Leah.

Leah lifted the glass and put it to her lips.

Chapter Fifty-Four

'This must be difficult...' Tate chewed some more egg.

Leah had a tiny amount of wine in her mouth. She replaced the glass on the table.

'...looking after someone who isn't the person they used to be.' He nodded to a photo, on the window ledge, of Leah and Olivia with their father when they were kids. The rainclouds had darkened the view of the garden beyond.

Leah watched him take a glug of her wine while he examined the picture. Had that been a trick? Was hers now the glass that was drugged?

'I hear it's like a death. Even though they're alive the person you knew is gone.'

'He's still my father.'

Tate met her eye. 'But you must often wish for a release.'

Leah knew what he was insinuating. 'No.'

'When you're exhausted and you need Saturday off, you must have thoughts you're not proud of.'

'He's still independent.'

'But for how much longer?'

'I don't ever think about that.'

'No? Don't consider how difficult it's going to become in the future, how he's going to drain the savings you've been putting away for yourself?'

'I only care about his wellbeing. I've had a drink with you now, tell me where he is.'

'That wasn't a drink. You barely wet your lips.' He took another gulp from his. 'Mine's going to need refilling in a moment. I hope you're not going to make me feel uncomfortable.' He waited, fork poised over his plate.

Leah picked up her glass and tipped it back against her lips. She took a little, swallowed as loudly as she could.

'Very commendable. What you were saying about your father ... that's not really the truth, is it? I'm sure it causes friction between you and Elliot.'

'What does it matter to you?'

Tate put down his glass, a look of approval on his face as if she'd asked precisely the right question. He filled his from the bottle, leaned across and filled hers almost to the brim. 'This – us – is an investment of time. All relationships are. My mistake in the past has been my inability to make an informed choice. It's something I have to remedy now. My energies *and time* have frequently been wasted on the wrong people. Through no fault of their own. But it causes resentment in me. A resentment I, unfortunately, have to satisfy.'

Was he really making it sound like an apology?

'I decided to kill Alice Booth a long time ago. The days and months that I lost yearning for a future with her, when she was patently the wrong person, irked me more than her rejection. But I had to be as good as my word. If I'm not, I don't really exist. I'm just a hapless lump of flesh at the mercy of others. My word is my will, my control.'

'So are you really going to be good as your word now? Are you lying about my father and Elliot?' She looked swiftly down at her knife and then up again.

'No. I promise, I've never lied to you.'

'You said you lived in Alice Booth's house.'

'That was your assumption.' He scraped his fork through his mayonnaise.

'You lied to the police. About giving yourself up.'

'But I didn't lie to you.' He quickly licked the back of his fork. 'You're not eating.'

'Just ask me what you need to know!' She immediately regretted the outburst.

Tate was impassive. 'So, the friction between you and Elliot, that makes the situation with your father even more difficult.'

Leah inhaled. 'No. That makes things between Elliot and me difficult.'

'Because your husband is selfish?'

Leah didn't respond.

Tate nodded. 'And demanding. Always has been but you've always rationalised his behaviour because he has a lot to put up with. The spectre of Olivia's death then your mother dying and now your father losing his mind.'

She bit her tongue. What hadn't he learned from Elliot?

'But when you shake it all down you realise that Elliot

285

has only been present for those events. He didn't actually support or help you.'

Leah's right hand slid from the table and into her lap.

'And on top of that he's been having an affair behind your back. Looking for his moment to escape you and the misery you've made him part of.'

'Is this what you do?' She had to distract him. 'Break down people's lives for fun?'

Tate looked genuinely affronted. 'People are easy to break down. They're such a rude construction. Not you though. That's why I want to help you. I want you to see things as clearly as I do. I heard Elliot and Katya outside your house last night. Valentine's night. The night you'd been in a road accident. Did he care about that? Or was he too busy trying to think of a way to tell you he doesn't love you anymore?'

Leah's palm moved to her right knee. She could feel the top of the mini crowbar poking through the denim.

'And your father is just as demanding. I imagine your mother was the one who kept the family together. But with her gone it's just you left to deal with two selfish men.'

Her fingers touched the two metallic points.

'In moments alone, every now and again, don't you wish them away?'

Leah shook her head.

'I've promised you I won't lie to you. I only ask you do the same in return.'

She gripped the metal hard. 'What have you done with them?'

Tate took another large swig of his wine. 'Food first.'

Chapter Fifty-Five

'A mouthful, just so my hard work isn't wasted. Then we talk about your father, I promise.'

Leah picked up her fork and jabbed it harshly into the egg on her plate.

'I'm sure he didn't teach you to eat like that.'

She met the mock remonstration in his expression, exhaled through her nose and then put the food past her lips.

Tate nodded satisfaction as she started to chew. 'He's not in this house but he's nearby.' He paused when she stopped eating and raised his eyebrows again.

Leah moved her jaw faster, the cool pulped egg turning to paste in her dry mouth.

'Likewise Elliot. If you don't behave though, you don't find them.'

'Are they alive?' Leah felt her throat close up

'Speaking with your mouth full? I'm sure your father would take a dim view of that too.'

Leah put down her fork.

'Yes, they are. But I need to know a few more details before I give you anymore.' He looked pointedly at the fork.

She picked it back up.

'Are you going to swallow?' His green eyes were on her lips now.

Leah briefly closed her eyelids and choked the egg down. Was that what he'd actually drugged?

Tate leaned further back in his chair. 'How badly did it affect your father? Losing Olivia? I know how it's afflicted you, what it did to your confidence when you were growing up.'

That wasn't a conversation she'd ever had with her father. 'What are you doing?'

'Getting to know you.'

'What has Elliot told you?'

'Exactly what I wanted to hear, I imagine. To be fair though, he did so under duress.'

'What did you do to him?' Leah felt sick as the food slid down to her stomach.

'I've told you, he's alive. Although I'm not sure you'll want that to remain the case.'

Leah clenched the fork firmly in her fist.

His gaze dropped to it. 'Thinking of using that? Or maybe the knife?'

She shook her head.

'We should really get that out of the way, if you're planning to.'

Leah's breath whistled from her nose a few times before she dropped it noisily onto the plate.

'You've finished then?'

'If you really knew me, you'd know that I love my father...'

'And Elliot? You love him?'

'Yes.' But she paused a second before carrying on. 'Yes,' she repeated.

He narrowed his eyes. 'Not entirely convincing. Did you know that Katya wasn't his first infidelity?'

Leah nodded, maintaining eye contact, but knew she hadn't sold the lie.

'Gaynor, Allegra, Nicola, you're familiar with those names?'

She nodded again, feeling her insides collapse.

'He was seeing Allegra three months after you got married. If you knew about it, that shows great forbearance on your part.' Tate sipped his wine while he allowed her to digest what he'd told her. 'And a complete disregard for you on his.'

She suspected it was the truth. But how had he extracted those names from Elliot?

'I don't want him to come to harm,' she said very deliberately. 'I never want that.'

Tate nodded thoughtfully. 'Message received.' He chewed his lip thoughtfully. 'I just wonder what it would take to convince you that disposing of him is the best thing that could happen to you.'

'Nothing,' she said definitively. Leah watched his expression turn blank. She realised she had to leave herself something to negotiate with. 'You're right though. I don't love him anymore.'

A vague spark flickered in his eyes.

'It's been over for a long time between us and, until recently, I've been in denial of that.' It wasn't hard for Leah to sell the truth.

Surprise on his face now, as if they'd made a breakthrough. 'You valued him above yourself?'

She nodded agreement.

'Even though he was conspiring to leave you.'

It's because of Olivia that you don't value yourself. Because you wish that it had been you hit by the car.'

Leah froze.

'Elliot told me how you've carried it. But did it ever occur to you that he used that to abuse you in the way he has?'

She'd only ever shared that guilt with Elliot. Her breathing quickened.

'Cynically using the fact that you feel worthless because you're convinced you're to blame for your sister's death.'

Chapter Fifty-Six

Leah's eyes were fixed on Tate's lips, the mouth of a stranger uttering things she could barely admit to herself.

'It was your frisbee she ran into the road to collect. How could you *not* feel that way?'

She experienced a familiar sensation. Those bruises of grief and anger that were always there aching in her stomach again. She was at the roadside, touching her sister's warm face before her father dragged her away. It was the last time she'd seen Olivia. She couldn't picture her expression but remembered the last heat of her skin against her palm.

'Elliot told me that you can never forgive yourself. Is that why you can always forgive *him*?'

Despite how desperate she was to know if Elliot was safe, however Tate had learnt it, it still felt like another betrayal.

'I found a couple of steaks in the fridge. How do you like yours cooked?'

Leah's hands shot to the cutlery in front of her as soon as Tate rose.

He regarded her with affectionate amusement. 'Medium, rare? These are the little details I need to know.' He dumped his napkin on the table and picked up his empty plate. He leaned over and took hers. 'I'll let you collect yourself but I'll keep this door open so we can talk.'

Leah felt him breeze past her and flinched, but he carried on to the kitchen. She heard him put the plates on the side, the gas ring firing up and a pan clanging onto it.

'If you want to help out, fill our glasses.'

Leah's eyes shifted to the bottle. Could she knock him unconscious with it? Her gaze flitted about the room. Anything else she could use as a weapon? There were only books and photos. She turned in the direction of the kitchen door and expected to find him watching her from there. He wasn't.

'You didn't answer my question,' he called from the stove.

'Very well done.' She had to keep him busy out there. Without taking her eyes from the doorway she put her hand to the crowbar. Could she slide it out in time?

He appeared in the kitchen doorway. 'I'm blue so I'll do mine first and let it rest so I can focus on yours.'

She nodded.

'I've salvaged a salad from the drawer. Slim pickings but the meat's the star.' He was gone again.

As soon as she heard the sizzle of steak hitting the skillet she leaned forward and started rolling up the right leg of her jeans.

'How are we on the wine?'

'Nearly there.' She exposed the top of the crowbar, which meant she could pull it out of her boot. She tugged it clear and placed it on the floor under the table. Then she frantically rolled her trouser leg down again.

'You sound suddenly compliant. What are you up to?'

As Tate walked back into the room Leah was on her feet. She grabbed the bottle from his side of the table and started filling his glass. She turned towards him.

Tate just nodded, audited the cutlery on the table and stepped back into the kitchen. 'Won't be long. D'you know if your father has any English mustard?'

Leah sat but angled her chair so her back wasn't square to the door. It creaked as she did so. 'Might be some in the cupboard above the fridge.'

'You're moving about.'

She turned to find him standing in the doorway again. 'I don't want my back to you.'

'Because it's rude?' He smirked and quickly disappeared.

Had he seen the crowbar on the carpet? Leah put her boot on it and shoved it further forward. But whatever she had on hand to attack him with she couldn't use it until he'd told her where her father and Elliot were.

'Nothing for you to do except sip the wine,' he said significantly.

Her glass was still full, but she wasn't about to drink it. As the bottle had been shared between them she hoped it hadn't been drugged but what about the mouthful of food he'd made her eat? She didn't feel drowsy yet. Leah scanned the room again. How else could she use this window of time? Had he foreseen everything she might try or was he positive she wouldn't attempt anything when two lives were at stake? He hadn't offered her any proof that either of them was alive. Perhaps he was just getting off on tormenting Leah before he killed her too.

She had to wait. Had to believe that he would reward her for obeying him. What else could she do? Leah picked up the knife and fork and clenched them tight in her sweaty palms.

In the kitchen the sickening fizzle intensified, filling her ears and merging with the hissing sound already there. The smell of cooked steak wafted in and the aroma was overpowering.

'Good to go,' he announced minutes later.

Leah tensed herself and turned her body towards the door as he entered with a plate in each hand and a bowl resting on his arm. She had the knife ready, could jab it into his stomach while both his hands were occupied. But it wasn't a sharp blade.

Tate paused and quickly took in her situation, as if expecting something to be out of place. Satisfied it wasn't, he arced around her to return to his side of the table. He put his own china plate down first. His sealed steak had a serrated, wooden-handled steak knife beside it. He retrieved the salad bowl from his arm, put it between them and then deposited her steak in front of her.

Beside it was another serrated steak knife.

'All yours,' he declared.

Leah looked down at it, the smell hitting her in the face as she considered the significance of what he'd given her.

Tate seated himself and replaced the napkin in his lap. He nodded at his steak. 'Your father knows how to live.'

Leah looked up at him, the sizzling still in her ears.

Tate picked up his fork and serrated knife and started energetically sawing through the meat.

Chapter Fifty-Seven

Leah regarded the puddle of red under the piece of meat on her plate.

'D'you think your father blamed you for Olivia's death?'

Leah heard his fork scrape over his teeth and him chew vigorously. 'When are you going to tell me where he is?' She didn't look up.

'As soon as we've had a pass at this course,' he said placatingly through a mouthful. 'Shame I couldn't find any mustard, this is excellent.'

Leah took hold of the steak knife.

'Good. Just one bite.'

There was something sprinkled over the meat. Was it salt or had he drugged it? It was far from well done. The puddle of red was expanding underneath as the meat relaxed. She sawed a small corner off it.

'Elliot told me that your father calls you Olivia now. She died when she was nine. That's plenty of time for you to replace her as his favourite, isn't it?'

Leah didn't respond but managed to separate the morsel from the main steak.

'But it doesn't sound like you have. Is that because you were the older sister who should have been looking out for her? Has he not forgiven you for that?'

Leah examined the meat on her fork.

'Done OK for you?'

The idea of putting it in her mouth seemed repugnant. Leah breathed through her mouth so she couldn't smell it.

'Wouldn't you prefer that guilt to be gone now? Isn't your father just a constant reminder of something you'd rather forget?'

She shook her head.

'And Elliot, he's the only one you've told. And he's used it against you. Abused it so he can be unfaithful without reproach.'

Leah put the fork to her mouth, but her lips wouldn't open.

'Year after year, knowing deep down you were unhappy but not thinking you were worthy of anything better.'

She tried to block out his words, concentrate on what she had to do.

'You've convinced yourself you're as happy as you're ever entitled to be, deceiving nobody but you that you have a loveless marriage worth salvaging. But what if you could start again?'

Chew and swallow. But it seemed like an insurmountable task.

'Wipe all that guilt and negativity away. Start afresh as Leah Talbot and not the sister who should have died on the road. I can see who you are. They never have. They've broken you down for something that wasn't your fault. And you've taken it for too long.'

Leah slid the piece of meat into her mouth and chewed quickly.

Tate was silent as her teeth worked it. He watched her with fascination.

Leah swallowed it.

He picked up his wine glass and sipped. 'You can change. Look what you're capable of. I know you're a vegetarian.'

Leah tried not to react as she felt the bolus of meat sink inside her.

'Can't you see why we're sitting here together? You had your own accident on the road, but you survived. Surely you must acknowledge the significance of that? You came to me with blood on your hands and we both experienced an undeniable connection. You believe you killed your sister. *They* already suspect you did. Might they be right? Are you already a killer?'

Leah held his green eyes. 'One bite. It's done. Take me to them.'

Tate nodded but seemed unsure. 'Think you're ready?'

Leah's hands were shaking. They still held the cutlery.

Tate's eyes dipped to them. 'Leave the fork here.'

She dropped it onto the table.

Tate emptied his wine glass. 'It's just us here now. We have as much time as we need for this.'

Leah stood but the room lurched.

Tate remained seated, studying her.

'Did you drug me?'

He pursed his lips and shook his head. 'I think you're just a little overcome.'

She slid her foot forward to steady herself. It didn't connect with the crowbar. But she still had the serrated knife in her hand.

Tate took his napkin from his lap, dabbed his lips and tossed it on the table. 'You can come at me with that if you want. I'm unarmed. Is that what you'd like to do?'

'No.'

'No because you're scared or no because I've never done anything to harm you?'

'You said you wouldn't lie to me, take me to them.'

'And I will. I just want to make sure you realise there's a reason you haven't planted that blade in me yet.' He stood up slowly, his chair sliding out behind him.

Leah took two paces back. She was getting further away from the crowbar.

Tate fumbled in his pocket and took out a small set of keys. He held them up.

Leah recognised them. They were to the dilapidated stone outbuilding at the rear of the property that used to be the apple store for the press.

He threw the keys over to her side of the table. 'You lead the way.'

Chapter Fifty-Eight

Was this a trap? Leah half turned to the door but swivelled back again.

Tate was still standing in the same position on his side of the table. He raised his palms. 'I don't have a weapon. This is your choice now.'

Leah scraped up the keys from the table with her empty left hand.

Tate's expression didn't shift. He watched her with breathless interest.

'They're still alive? You can't lie to me.'

'I promise, they're alive for as long as you need them to be.'

She backed away a few more paces until she bumped into the doorjamb.

'I'll follow you out. The back door is open.'

Leah regarded the cutlery in front of him. He could easily pick up his knife and pounce. She slid past the doorjamb so she was standing in the hallway with the kitchen door to her right.

'I've been making all the right decisions on your behalf.' He leaned forward and snuffed out the five candles of the candelabra by pinching them with his fingertips. 'Now it's your turn. Go. I'll join you now.'

Leah turned and strode quickly through the kitchen. The smell of cooking was heavy and the atmosphere smoky. She reached the back door and gripped the handle. No key. She couldn't leave and lock it from the outside. She opened it inward.

Turning back she saw no sign of Tate in the hallway. She stepped through the door and the cold evening doused her face. The last of the golden sunlight was just disappearing. Leah stumbled along the wet paving-stone path, past the garage, and headed towards the half-collapsed stone structure fifty yards beyond it, her irregular breaths clouding around her. There were no other properties within shouting distance. Nobody would be able to hear.

She stopped and glanced back at the house. Through the window of the back door she couldn't see Tate in the kitchen. Her eyes shifted to the lit window of the dining room. He was no longer standing at his side of the table.

Leah staggered on towards the apple store. It had always been too damp to keep anything but tools in there. Were Elliot and her father really imprisoned inside? As she approached, she took in the battered blue doors and the collapsed roof which sagged inwards at the middle.

Her fingers trembled as she tried to maintain her grip on the knife and insert the first key into the rusted padlock securing the doors. Fragments fell out as she waggled it and pushed harder. 'Come on.' She looked back and saw Tate closing the back door behind him.

Leah pushed the key all the way in and twisted it. The padlock opened and she took it from the hooks and allowed it to fall into the mud.

Tate's footfalls made her spin back in his direction. He was striding in her direction, his eyes on hers.

Leah pulled open the doors and let the failing daylight into the interior.

The first face she recognised was her father's. He was sitting on a black metal garden chair. He was gagged with a length of green plastic hosepipe and the same held his hands to the arms and bound his ankles together. 'Dad!'

His features were deathly pale, and his blue eyes rolled sluggishly up at her.

Then Leah saw Elliot. He was seated on another metal chair and bound by the same. But his face was a mask of dark dried blood.

It felt like the breath had been sucked out of her chest and her hand went to her mouth.

There were deep cuts to his face and Leah knew what Tate had used to make them. His jeans had been scored, the material slashed multiple times. There were incisions on the backs of his hands and the arms of his tan shirt were threadbare and saturated red.

'Elliot!'

His head was on one side, his eyes closed and there was no reaction to her exclamation.

She went to her father first, attempting to loosen the

plastic gag that was cutting so severely into the sides of his mouth. The knots at the back were too tight. Could she saw through them? Her gaze shot to the door and she could see that Tate was only about five paces away from the apple store. 'Stay away!' She brandished the knife.

Tate halted and held up both his hands.

'I'll kill you!'

'This is an understandable response,' he said calmly.

'I swear I will!' She held the blade out to him.

He nodded. 'But isn't this an overreaction?'

Leah dragged her father back in the chair. Could she close the doors? She quickly took in the rusted tools hanging on hooks on the stone wall opposite her. There was a hoe, a rake, a long wire brush. Nothing sharp.

'Haven't I already prepared you for this?'

Her focus darted back to where Tate was still standing.

'Katya, your nosy neighbours, Lownes; you've seen them all in the last twenty-four hours. Haven't I desensitised you to this now?'

'Elliot!' She turned to him but he didn't stir.

'He's lost a lot of blood. I spent more time with him than I did your father. Got to know a lot about you through my chats with him.'

Leah's eyes bounced between them. Was Elliot dead? His eyelids were stuck down with dried blood.

'But considering he was your husband, I was done with him surprisingly quickly. Elliot didn't really know you, did he? Didn't care to know you, only what you could do for him.'

Leah's father grunted as he tried to move.

'Just sit tight.' Tate addressed him. 'This won't take long.'

Leah got in front of the chair so she was blocking her father. 'Stay back!' She arced the blade in front of the doorway.

'I will, as long as you need me to. I promise.'

'Elliot!'

Still no response. But with both of them tied up she had to defend them from Tate alone.

'Listen to me. Try to breathe. Try to calm down. This calls for a substantial paradigm shift. But I'm going to talk you through it. We'll get through this together.'

Chapter Fifty-Nine

Again, Leah considered slamming the doors and leaning her weight on them.

'I've told you, I won't try to come inside.' He'd read her mind. 'You'll be shut away in the dark with them and then what?'

'If you leave now, I promise I won't call the police.' But she knew the offer was as futile as the first time she'd made it.

'I've no intention of leaving. Not when we've made such progress.'

'Progress?' She spat scornfully.

'Your father…'

Leah didn't move from her protective position in front of him.

'I think he's having difficulty.' Tate's gaze was on him.

Leah turned the steak knife around in her hand, so she was holding it like a dagger. She brandished it at face

307

height, the blade protruding from her fist. She knew she'd have no hesitation in stabbing him if he came at her.

But he remained where he was.

Her father retched behind her.

'I think you've got him overexcited,' Tate declared.

But she still didn't move.

'Bear in mind, he doesn't know who I am. Doesn't know who you are.'

Leah could hear her father groaning against the gag.

'He hardly knows who he is let alone what he's doing here. If you stab me he won't be happy or sad. And if he *is* briefly relieved you saved his life, he won't even remember your name in a few minutes' time.'

Leah stepped quickly back so she was beside her father and could look at him.

His fearful eyes bulged and swivelled between the two of them.

'Maybe he thinks you're Olivia. Perhaps that's who he'd prefer to save him now, even though she's been gone for so long. Despite the fact you've tried to do everything in your power to fill her space.'

She had to release the gag, but she couldn't afford to take her eyes off Tate. 'Dad, try to breathe slowly.'

'He's been waiting for her to walk through the door all this time. But it's not going to happen. You're never going to be the daughter he wants to see.'

Leah's father arched his back as he tried to rise from the garden seat.

'You're holding that knife to the wrong person.' Tate's tone was calm.

'Dad, breathe in through your nose.'

But he continued to buck and struggle against his bonds.

'This is how he suffocates every day. Confusion and fear is all he knows now. Is that really the life you want for him?'

'Dad, it's OK. You have to keep still.'

But he kept squirming.

'I imagine he's never mistreated you. Tried to protect you from what happened. But you've always picked up on that quiet disappointment. He's been grieving for so long and now, every time you tell him you're not Olivia, it's like he's finding out she's dead for the very first time.'

'Shut up! Dad, I'm going to untie you now. Try to calm down.'

'Let him go. If he was still the father you knew, you know he'd want an end to this.'

Leah put her free hand on her father's shoulder.

'And don't *you* need an end to this? Every weekend watching a man trapped in a mouse wheel. Those moments of clarity, when he knows who you are and what you do for him, shrinking away, learning that his wife and favourite daughter are dead over and over again?'

'It won't work,' she barked at him. 'Whatever you're trying to do…'

'Put the knife in him,' he said collectedly. 'It's been a long day for him. A long day for you. You both need that relief now. You both deserve it.'

Leah's father moaned through the gag.

'What would you want if you were in his position? I know what choice I'd make.'

'Dad, I'll free you now.' Her voice trembled. 'Just wait…'

'For what? I think you're more afraid of the consequences than actually doing it. I'll take responsibility if you want. You can say you found them both butchered here.'

'If you want to help me! Go!' she yelled, her throat grating each word.

'I can do it for you.'

Leah tugged in a breath.

'Is that what you want me to say?'

Her father bucked in the chair.

'It is, isn't it?'

'Stay the fuck away from him!'

'Give me the knife.' He extended his hand. 'You know I'm not going to harm *you*. Give me the knife.'

'Take one step....'

'No.' Tate took a pace forward. 'You won't do that.'

Leah's father shouted aggressively through the hose, his anger directed at Tate.

'He knows I'm a threat. He's defending you. Maybe he thinks you're Olivia.'

Leah's leg muscles stiffened as she prepared to launch herself at Tate but then another voice started screaming behind her.

Chapter Sixty

Leah didn't shift her attention from Tate. It was Elliot. He was alive. A small gap of relief opened in her, but the revelation didn't negate the danger she was in. Elliot was tied as securely as her father.

'Looks like somebody's decided to step up to the mark.' Tate's eyes were over Leah's shoulder. 'Better late than never.'

'You promised you wouldn't come inside.' Leah was still poised to launch herself at Tate.

'I did. And I won't. I think you might need my help now though, but I won't enter until you invite me to.'

Elliot yelled against his gag again.

'You can't really complain about your predicament, Elliot.' Tate said past Leah. 'You told me about this place. You led me here. And you didn't need a lot of inducement either.'

'Elliot.' Leah didn't dare look in his direction.

He kept screaming.

311

'Elliot!'

He stopped.

She guessed the pain of his wounds must be overwhelming. 'Can you get free?'

Tate's face was impassive. As if he knew how the conversation was about to go.

Leah heard Elliot struggle and the hose creaking as he moaned in agony.

'He doesn't need to do that. Put himself through any more trauma. Neither of them does.'

'Try to get loose, Elliot.'

He breathed erratically and a sob escaped his nostrils.

Tate sighed slightly. 'You're expecting too much of him. Elliot, you can stop now. It's a waste of your time and ours.'

She could hear Elliot's movement continue but quickly decrease.

'When has he ever put himself on the line for you? When has he ever done anything but look out for himself? Think that's going to change in circumstances like this?'

Leah's father twisted his bound hands.

'But look at you, prepared to kill for them both. Do either of these gentlemen deserve your loyalty? What have they done to make you risk your life for them?'

'Step back.' Leah tightened her fist on the knife handle.

He didn't. 'Do you believe Elliot thought of you when he was sleeping with Katya or Gaynor or Allegra or Nicola? Happily making a mockery of your marriage time and time again? Do you know how easily he gave up those details to save himself, not realising that each cut I gave him was a punishment and not an incentive to give me more.'

'I told you, I don't love him anymore.' Was this what he needed to be told again or was she condemning Elliot to death by saying she no longer cared for him?

'So you said. But do you feel so worthless that you're going to let him get away with it?'

'I don't want to see him again,' she retorted but Tate's reaction made Leah seal her mouth tight.

His satisfaction was plainly visible. 'And why did he get away with it for so long? Who made you feel so worthless?'

She didn't look at her father. Kept her eyes unblinking on Tate's.

'What comfort was Elliot to you on Valentine's night? You could have died in that crash. Would he have been concerned, or would he have seen that as a very convenient way out? He wouldn't have had to confront you about Katya then, as she wanted him to last night. Do you think he cared that you sat alone on the floor in your shower for so long?'

Abhorrence broke through her. She knew he'd been in the house but now there was no doubt he'd seen her there, thinking about Olivia and how the accident of so many years before had been the catalyst for the person she'd become, living in a house with a husband who didn't love her.

'That's why you came to see me again this morning. It was the first time you'd exerted your will in a long time. And you found that that's exactly what I'd done with Alice Booth. Taken back the control she took from me years before. You can exert your will again. I think you're capable but saying the word to me is exactly the same.'

'No. I don't want this!'

'You want to punish Elliot.' His voice remained even. 'And you never want to see him again.'

'Don't twist my words. You've harmed him enough.'

'Enough for what? All the years of deception or for handing me the key to your insecurities?'

Leah's father and Elliot were both noisily fighting to get free.

'Say the word and it's done. No repercussions.'

Leah shook her head.

'Say it!'

'You're the only one I want dead!'

'Because I'm the only one telling the truth!' Tate took another step forward.

'Stay back!' Leah noticed her father had stopped moving. 'Dad!' But she couldn't afford to look down at him, even for a second.

There was no response. Elliot continued struggling behind her.

'Dad!'

'I think he's fitting.' Tate squinted.

'Dad!'

'Perhaps this decision's about to be made for you.' He didn't look up.

Leah shot a glance to her father. His body was taut and she could only see the whites of his eyes.

Chapter Sixty-One

'It appears, despite my best efforts, you can't decide for yourself.' Tate regarded Leah's father as his body jerked in the chair.

She had to cut him free of his gag, but she couldn't afford to take her eyes off Tate.

'If you really think he's worth saving...'

Leah put her free hand to the hose wrapped around his head, but it was bound too tight. It had to be cut.

'...which you obviously do, I won't stop you. Go ahead.' There was disapproval in his voice.

She shook her head. Another trick?

Her father noisily drew air in around the gag.

'I told you, I won't lie to you. Release him. Give him the shell of his life back. Even if dying now is what's best for him.'

Leah lowered her blade and slid the blunt side under the hose at the side of her father's face. She started furiously sawing away from his cheek.

'The serrated edge should make short work of that.'

She focused on cutting through the plastic, Tate lingering at the periphery of her vision. He could attack her now and she would never slide the steak knife back out in time to defend herself.

The blade got traction on the double thickness of hose.

'But if you choose one man you forfeit the other.'

Her hand halted.

'I'm making that decision on your behalf. It really would be remiss of me to watch you throw this opportunity away.'

Her father's eyes had closed, his convulsions were weakening.

'Dad!' Leah started sawing again. She had to save him first. 'I refuse to make that choice.'

'You're incapable of resolving this. You'll thank me though. That's if your father isn't already braindead.'

'Stay with me, Dad!' The knife was through the first coil.

As she sawed faster her father's head bounced loosely on his neck.

'Look how close you are. You could just wait a few seconds. Keep sawing, if you like though, so you can tell yourself you tried.'

'Shut up!' The blade was cutting through the second coil. She got her fingers under the hose and opened up a gap. 'Breathe, Dad!'

'Maybe he doesn't want to anymore. Perhaps there's a part of him that wants this as much as you.'

She sawed frantically and Tate watched, motionless.

The coil severed and Leah pulled the plastic away from his face. 'Dad?' She shook him.

His head lolled forward.

'Dad!' She lifted his chin and slapped his cheek.

His eyes flickered under his lids.

'Take a breath!'

After a second, his chest suddenly heaved and he noisily dragged in air.

Leah turned to Tate. He was still watching silently. When she stole a look at her father his bloodshot eyes were open, uncomprehending.

'What is this?' Spittle ran down his chin.

'It's all right, Dad, you're OK.'

Her father squinted at Tate and then blinked as he tried to focus his eyes on her. 'What are you doing?'

'D'you think he recognises you?'

'It's Leah. This man tied you up.'

Her father bounced his gaze fearfully between them.

Leah's fingers trembled as she tried to release his left hand from the arm of the chair, but the hose was binding it tight.

'Cut them. I'm not going to stop you.' Tate promised. 'Soon have you out.' He addressed her father.

Leah couldn't get the knife under the coils.

'Just saw down.' Tate suggested. 'Careful not to sever any of his main cables though.'

Leah looked into her father's confused expression to reassure him, but she could see he was just as wary of her as he was of Tate. 'It's me. It's Leah. I'm going to get you out of here.'

'Maybe he would rather it was Olivia who was helping him.'

Leah sawed the blade above his wrist.

Elliot started yelling through his gag again.

Leah's father swivelled his head to where he was. He turned back to her, eyes widening.

'I think Elliot is becoming concerned about the choice you've made.'

'I haven't made any choice!' Her arm worked furiously.

'It's not too late. You can still change your mind.'

'What is he talking about?' There was still no recognition in her father's eyes.

'Your daughter has to choose you or her husband. You remember Elliot?'

'Just keep still, Dad.' She had to cut him loose. Give him a chance to defend himself if Tate attacked her.

Elliot kept screaming.

But under it Leah could still hear Tate observe:

'Looks like she's just made up her mind, Elliot.'

Chapter Sixty-Two

Ragged ends of hose flicked up as Leah's knife cut through them. She yanked on the remaining length and it came away. 'Dad, use your hand to free the other one.'

He regarded her with bewilderment.

But his feet were still tied. And even if he could get out of the chair it was unlikely he could defend himself. 'Don't!'

Tate had advanced a step.

Leah held up the blade to him again.

His expression remained impassive. 'See to your father.'

'Keep back!' She swiped the steak knife. 'I mean it.'

'I've no doubt you do. In fact, I'm probably the only man here who doesn't underestimate you.'

'I can't move my legs,' her father whimpered.

'See to him. Take him back up to the cottage. I'll finish here.' Tate's gaze switched to Elliot.

Elliot slid noisily back in his chair.

Leah swung the blade again as he took another pace forward.

'Who else here has shown you the consideration that I have? I've laid it out for you. Made it as easy as possible. My instincts are good. I refuse to believe I've been wasting my time.'

'Dad, try to untie yourself.' Her eyes were on Tate but she could see her father made no move to free his other hand.

Elliot grunted and rocked in his chair.

'I could have dealt with both these problems before you arrived, but I didn't want to be presumptuous.'

'Don't.' She raised the knife high as he approached.

He was a couple of feet inside the apple store. 'You have the potential, Leah Talbot, but it needs to be harnessed.'

'By you? What is it you believe will happen after this?' She had to play for time. Distract him while she weighed up non-existent options

'Enlightenment,' he replied, as if it were obvious.

'And then what? My gratitude?' She retorted caustically.

'Your life is about to change for the better. You may not see it now as I do but once a situation becomes academic the only path left will be the right one.' He extended his hand. 'Make the right choice and join me.'

Leah brought the blade down and it caught the pads of his fingers.

He snatched them back, pain briefly registering on his face. He examined the cut.

Leah caught her breath, could see drops of blood welling up on his middle finger.

Tate seemed to check himself before he inhaled. 'Let me have the knife now.'

There was a clatter from behind Leah. She didn't turn but guessed Elliot had tipped over in his chair.

Tate briefly looked down at the floor. 'First time he's fallen at your feet?'

'Stay away from her.'

The silence that briefly followed underscored the threat.

Leah looked down at her father. He was glaring at Tate.

'Leave my daughter alone.' He didn't blink.

'Is this a breakthrough?' Tate sucked his fingers. 'This girl you're valiantly protecting though, can you tell me her name?'

The hose securing Leah's father's other hand creaked as his body tensed.

'Can you? Tell me who she is.'

Her father's jaw clenched, the muscles throbbing in his jaw.

'Don't answer him, Dad.'

'What about your wife, will she remember? Should I go and get her? D'you think she'll jog your memory for you?'

Leah's father's eyes burnt, full of an intensity she hadn't seen for a long time.

'Is she indisposed?'

Leah's knuckles went white along the handle of the knife.

'Take these off.' Leah's father nodded at his remaining bonds. 'Take these off and let me out of this chair.'

'Looks like he's coming to your defence.'

'That's enough.'

Tate seemed satisfied by the barely controlled rage in Leah's growl.

Squeaking and thudding as Elliot writhed on the floor.

Tate raised his palm at Leah's father. 'Just give me her name.'

'Dad—'

Her father lifted his hand too. Like he used to when she was a little girl, irked at her interruption. He didn't wrench his attention from Tate. 'Olivia,' he whispered, his expression triumphant.

Leah lunged with the blade.

Chapter Sixty-Three

L eah gasped and held up both her empty hands.

Tate was open mouthed too.

Leah's father breathed heavily down his nose.

'You chose.' Tate stated but both words were whispered, almost in awe.

Her eyes were on the blade and where it was buried.

Elliot had stopped struggling.

'Olivia,' her father said.

Tate looked down, his chin grazing the top of the blade. The metal was half buried at the bottom of his neck, just above his clavicle. The motion prompted blood to pour from the wound.

Leah hadn't aimed for any particular part of Tate's chest. Her palms went to her lips as he reeled unsteadily. She couldn't allow the shock of what she'd done to paralyse her.

There was surprise on his face as he carefully took hold of the wooden handle.

Leah's fingertips were under her eyes.

He focussed on her, opened his mouth to speak but gagged.

'Untie yourself, Dad.'

Tate gurgled as blood flowed faster from the deep slit. His expression changed, shifted to triumph.

Her father hadn't moved.

'Quickly!'

She heard him tugging at the piping around his other wrist.

Elliot was saying something incoherent through his gag.

Tate yanked out the knife.

Leah drew breath the same time as he did but his bubbled.

Tate staggered back, his hand to the wound but blood pouring through his fingers.

'You left me no choice.' Leah didn't blink.

His gaze slid sideways. He was looking at the wall opposite. Staggering to it, he placed his palms on the bricks, his back to her.

She kept her attention firmly on him. 'Hurry,' she addressed her Dad. Then she backed over to where Elliot was lying on the floor on his left side.

He was still babbling at her through the gag.

She worked at the tight knots securing his right hand to the chair arm, dropping her eyes to her trembling fingers and then returning them to Tate.

Tate's body sagged and he leaned harder against the wall. Blood was pooling in droplets at his feet. Had he brought a weapon out with him?

The knots were so tight and Elliot was struggling and tensing the hose.

'Keep still!' she hissed. 'Let me do it.'

Her father had his other hand clear and bent unsteadily forward to his bound ankles.

As Leah worked frantically on Elliot's bonds, Tate went down onto one knee.

Leah's father was bent all the way forward now, grunting as he fought to untie his legs.

Leah released Elliot's hand and checked Tate. He was still motionless. She uncoiled the hose and her husband's hand started working on his other. She concentrated on his feet.

Tate tried to stand again but dropped down hard onto both knees.

Leah picked at the knots and noticed he'd dropped the steak knife. It was at the bottom of the wall.

Elliot used both hands to tug at the hose around his face.

Her father had his feet loose and tried to stand up. He collapsed back into his chair.

'Dad, wait there. We'll help you up now.' She undid the knot at the back of Elliot's head, and he ripped it away.

Tate's body collapsed against the wall.

Leah helped Elliot with his ankles.

'I'm sorry.' Were her husband's first words.

'Can you get up?' She pulled the chair away from him.

Elliot took a few breaths and nodded. He started to stand but trembled and flinched as the motion emphasized every slice in his muscles.

Leah supported him to his feet.

His eyes looked so white in the dark blood mask of his face and he opened his sticky lips to speak again.

'Save your energy. Can you walk?'

He nodded and she guided him to where her father was trying to rise a second time.

'Your dad,' Elliot whispered and took his arm from Leah.

She helped him out of the chair then took a few cautious paces towards Tate.

'Don't,' Elliot warned.

She halted but quickly raced forward and scraped up the knife.

Tate didn't react.

'Let's go,' Elliot whisper-yelled.

In the dregs of daylight Leah could see a small puddle of dark blood between Tate's knees as it broke its tension and flowed backwards, picking up dust as it went.

'We can't leave him like this,' Leah's father said.

'We'll call him an ambulance.' But Leah knew it would probably be too late.

'Come on.' Elliot dragged her father out of the apple store.

Leah took one more look at Tate's hunched shoulders and followed them.

'We get inside, lock the doors and call the police.' Elliot was determinedly walking her father back to the cottage, their breath misting around them.

She caught up with them. 'Careful, Dad's about to collapse.' She took his other arm.

But Elliot wouldn't slow down.

'Wait!' She stopped.

'What is it?' Elliot turned to her. Tears had welled up in his eyes and were trickling white tracks down his face.

'He has Dad's phone. And mine.' Leah turned back to the apple store.

Chapter Sixty-Four

Leah found the spare key and locked the back door as soon as they were inside the kitchen. She and Elliot helped her father through to the hallway and she double checked that the phone wasn't there. Tate had it and her mobile in his pocket but going back into the apple store was a bad idea.

'I just need to sit down,' her father declared.

'No time.' She repositioned herself under his arm. 'We'll drive my car to the nearest neighbour, call the police and an ambulance.'

Elliot nodded and blanched as he took her father's weight. 'Can you walk OK now?'

Leah's father looked ashen. 'If I can just have a minute's rest.'

Leah shook her head at Elliot. 'Come on.'

The three of them shuffled through the tight hallway towards the front door.

A rattling sound came from behind them.

They all stopped dead and Leah and Elliot turned in the direction of the noise.

The back-door handle was being jerked down.

'Out the front.' Leah was already dragging them both to the door. She opened it and they helped her father onto the path.

'Where are we going?' he asked bewildered.

Leah gripped the steak knife firmly in her right fist. 'He could come up the side of the house. Keep a lookout.' She fixed her eyes on the darkened track overhung by trees to her left as they headed up the short path to where her car was.

'I need my coat.'

Leah felt her father resist them. 'You don't need it. It'll be warm in the car.'

'Quiet,' Elliot snapped, his attention locked on the track to one side.

They'd reached the gate.

'Support him.' Leah took her arm from under her father and, watching the house, scrabbled in her pocket for the key.

'Hurry.' Elliot turned her father so he could look back as well.

No sign of it in either pocket. Maybe it was back in the house or had fallen out in the apple store. She tried her back pockets and felt metal. 'Got it.'

She pressed the button and the door clunked.

'He's coming!' Elliot exclaimed.

Leah spotted Tate emerging from the shadows at the right side of the house. He was illuminated as he stumbled in front of the lights from the windows. He was carrying a long pole.

'Run!' Elliot turned to Leah in alarm.

'Dad can't outrun him. Get him inside the car.'

Elliot looked as if he was in two minds about releasing him and then nodded. 'Open the door!'

Leah lifted the handle of the passenger door, but it was locked. The car had been open. She'd just locked it again. She pressed the fob again and yanked the door. 'Put him in the back.'

Elliot was already shoving her father inside.

Leah knew she had to use the knife again. She turned back to the house, but Tate had already arrived.

He swung the implement in his hand. It was a rake and the edge of the heavy metallic teeth caught her in the left side of the jaw.

Leah was on the ground, white pulses of light in her eyes. She could hear Elliot shouting. And the knife was no longer in her hand. 'Dad!' She heard her voice scream, but it sounded like she was yelling in her own ear.

She had the key. They couldn't drive away. Leah was on her feet but slewed sideways and her face hit a wall.

A hand gripped her shoulder.

'Stay down. I'll finish here,' Tate's voice gurgled.

'Leah, get the knife!' Elliot cried.

Get up. Back on your feet.

Had she blacked out? She used the edge of the wall to haul herself up and turned. But the action seemed to continue and the struggle in front of her appeared to repeatedly zip by as if she were on a carousel.

331

Tate was climbing into the passenger side and she could hear Elliot.

'Get the fuck off us!'

Her eyes dropped to the ground. Where was the knife? But the dark dirt track lurched up at her and she put out her hands. Was she falling again? She staggered, directing herself at the car.

Her hands were around Tate's shoulders. The passenger door on the other side was open and her father was lying on his back on the ground. Elliot was half out, his torso on the dirt but his legs still inside.

Tate had hold of them and was trying to pull them back in.

'Let go of me! Leah, he's got the knife!'

Leah climbed onto his back and put her hands around his hot throat.

He tried to shake her off but as hard as she squeezed, he wouldn't let go of Elliot's legs. She slid her hand further down and found the wound in his throat. She put her two fingers inside its warm and moist interior.

Tate bucked underneath her, rose and slammed the back of his head into her face.

She was looking up at the car ceiling, realised she'd fallen and turned so she was lying on her spine between the back and front seats. Leah could hear Elliot's feet pedalling in Tate's grip, striking him in the face.

She hinged up and rolled over, preparing herself to jump on his back again, but her shin smarted as she put her weight on it and against something solid. She reached for it.

It was the wine bottle. She gripped it by the neck.

Leah straddled Tate and brought the bottle down on the back of his head as hard as she could. It clunked and she felt the full impact reverberate painfully in her wrist. She hit him with it again.

The third blow broke the bottle, but his hands were still on Elliot's thigh. Her father was motionless.

The jagged neck was still in her hand. 'Stop.'

He wasn't going to.

Leah fell onto his back and ground the bottleneck into the side of his neck.

Everything froze.

She pushed it further. Heard the glass crunch inside him.

Leah could smell the sweat in Tate's scalp, could feel his circulation pounding.

Pounding but gradually slowing.

As Elliot slid free, she waited there. Waited until Tate's heartbeat had weakened and stopped.

Leah didn't release him until the last clouds of his dying breath had floated away.

Chapter Sixty-Five

Leah didn't want to open her eyes. Sitting on the floor of the shower, the slight pressure of water on her scalp and knees, she clenched her shins a little tighter to herself and listened to the flow over her ears and the trickle into the plughole.

It was their first day home and they'd arrived mid-afternoon. She'd left Elliot perched on the edge of the couch flicking through the TV downstairs while she escaped to the bathroom.

They'd called in to see her father on their way from the hospital. He was the first to have been discharged and had insisted on going home. Leah had been against it but realised that, ironically, it was the one place where he felt secure. He'd already completely forgotten what had happened there.

He had his usual carer with him until Leah had packed some things and headed over later that evening. She was going to stay there with him for a few weeks and suspected she wouldn't be returning home.

She'd been treated for concussion and had remained in hospital while Elliot had been in the ICU. Thankfully, his face only needed six stitches, with a further fourteen on his torso. Most of the razor cuts Tate had made while he was torturing him would heal. Elliot's face was entirely concealed by bandages though.

Leah wondered if he was as glad of that as she was.

Did he resent her for ever knocking on Alice Booth's door? They hadn't begun to process the consequences of that, and every exchange they'd had since what had happened at her father's cottage had been about nothing but practicalities.

Once her father had been settled, once all the interviews with DI Byrne were over and they were finally approaching a semblance of normal life again, where would they begin on themselves? How far would they have to go back to find the point when it had fallen apart? Years before the deer on Plough Lane.

Here she was again, sitting in the shower, washing away the trauma of what had happened and thinking about Olivia and how her death had moulded the life she'd settled for. Martin Tate had effortlessly perceived that.

She opened her eyes and turned her head to the closed bathroom door as if he might be standing there again.

The droplets built up on her eyelashes and rolled down her face. She blinked them away, kept her gaze on the door. He'd wanted her to free herself. However repulsive his actions, he'd genuinely believed he was helping her. What had he planned for her beyond that? Was she simply the new promise he'd made to himself? His new purpose and hope after he'd dealt with his other failures? Maybe even the inhuman needed that too.

She could vividly recall the moment their lips had touched. What would have happened if she hadn't allowed it? But she was sure Tate would have brought mayhem into her and Elliot's life regardless. She could still feel his body stiffening as she held him and pushed the glass into his throat. She knew she would never be the same person again, even though that seemed like the actions of someone else entirely. A person Tate had extracted from her. Leah would remember that look of triumph on his face when she'd stabbed him as sharply as the sensation of his life ebbing away and the aroma of his scalp as he'd died underneath her. She'd had to do it, to save her father and Elliot. But why hadn't Tate finished Elliot? The knife had been in his hand.

Tate had easily abducted her husband on his walk to the station. Asked him to help him bump-start his car and led him to a car park before knocking him out. Did Elliot feel humiliated by that? But why had he been getting on a train if Katya lived a few streets away from their home? Was he really going to stay with a friend, or had it been Gaynor or Allegra or Nicola he was on his way to see? One infidelity was an affront to everything they'd built together but the notion that there were four women he'd been intimate with was something she still couldn't conceive of.

She wondered if he'd lied to them as much as he had to her. All this time Leah had lived with somebody she'd naively assumed she'd known. Some wounds would never heal. There was nothing left for her here. Had Martin Tate's intervention precipitated her acceptance of that?

Martin Tate wasn't his real name. The police were still trying to find out exactly who he was. They could start with Alice Booth. Trace him back to the person who'd been in love with her. Had it all been lies though? She suspected not. Everyone was a product of what was denied to them.

Her father had hidden it for decades. But as his personality was gradually eroded, he could no longer spare Leah from the hurt of their family loss. She had to honour all the years he'd done his utmost to spare her feelings, though, even if he hadn't always succeeded.

Leah stood and turned off the dial. It was good to be alone, however briefly. She dried herself and slipped on her towelling robe, deliberately busying her mind with the packing she had to do and making a mental inventory of what she would need to set up her office at her dad's cottage.

She walked barefoot onto the landing but paused on her way to the bedroom.

She could hear the noise of the TV downstairs, but something held her there. She opened her mouth but couldn't bring herself to call his name. Leah padded down the stairs.

She crossed the tiles and runner in the hallway and entered the lounge.

'Elliot.' Now she could say it.

Elliot was lying motionless on his back in the middle of the room.

She ran to him and knelt beside him. 'Elliot?' She shook him and his bandaged head fell to one side.

She took hold of his face and looked into his eyes. There was no life in them. She knew he was dead before she shook him again, tried to revive him and then checked his pulse.

His hand was outstretched. A glass of red wine had spilt along the oatmeal carpet and rolled against the leg of the sofa.

Leah looked over at the bottle on the table. This was Tate. She was certain of that. He'd orchestrated her presence at each crime scene he'd created, manipulated her the whole time. But now he was no longer the spectre she could point her finger at, who would believe that Leah didn't want to punish Elliot for all of the wrongs he'd done her?

Was that why Tate hadn't killed Elliot during their struggle in the car?

Elliot's eyes looked blankly at her from beneath the bandages on his face.

Leah took his hand. It was still warm. She was back at the roadside, touching the deer, touching her sister before her dad dragged her away. The warmth ebbing and her parents' love leaving with it.

She released Elliot, as if doing so could prevent what had been triggered again.

Chapter Sixty-Six

Three days and three hours earlier

Tate made his way along the track at the rear of Leah's house for the second time. In the morning light, he could see the stream on the left-hand side of the reeds clearly. There were ducks there, some of them on the bank, the others in the water.

There was nobody at the rear of Leah's place, so he paused at her gate and recalled watching her through the bathroom window and then going inside the house. He scolded himself for being so impetuous but the image of her sitting on the floor in the shower was still imprinted on his mind.

Some ducks quacked noisily behind him and he turned and spotted a hen surrounded by three drakes. They weren't too interested in her just yet. In spring they would be on her back, trying to mate and pecking her head until it was bald. He'd observed the brutality of that ritual before.

He was about to open Leah's gate when a thought occurred to him. He climbed over the fence to the stream and most of the ducks waddled away. One drake was defiant though and it was a drake he wanted. He grabbed the bird's body either side of its wings, his palms lightly compressing it through its fluffed-up feathers. It wasn't as plump as it looked, and it struggled a little, so he waited for it to realise it couldn't escape. Tate laid it on his chest and held it to his body with his left hand firmly over its neck.

With his free hand, he let himself into Leah's garden again and briefly surveyed it in the daylight. He'd watched her go out in the car after Elliot had left for his run. Skirting the overgrown lawn, he made for the passage at the right side of the house that he'd accessed the night before. When he reached the end of it, the hedge along the edge of the front drive concealed him completely.

He put his hand under the edge of the garage door and opened it sufficiently to slip under.

Again, he entered the kitchen through the side door of the garage. There he deposited the drake and it seemed unperturbed as it walked unsteadily across the tiles to the locked French doors.

When she found it, Tate wondered if Leah Talbot would understand the significance of the discovery, of a new drake imposing itself on the territory.

Then he saw the bottle of red wine on the counter next to the bowl of red and green peppers. About a quarter of it was missing and the lid had been replaced. Could he?

Tate took the syringe out of his jacket pocket and removed the cap from the needle. There was a full cylinder of yellowish liquid. A small amount of it was tasteless. He'd planned to administer it to Alice Booth to allow him to work on her but it hadn't been necessary.

Tate unscrewed the bottle lid and depressed the plunger into the wine.

He knew Leah didn't like red. Only one person was likely to drink this.

A double dose for Elliot. In fact, may as well empty the syringe. Tate replaced the lid, put the cap back on the needle and slipped it into his jacket.

Would Elliot be alone when he died here? Would he know that he'd lost Leah, that her new life would never again include Mr Absentee Valentine?

He considered how he would abduct Elliot and take him to the old pig farm. Maybe he'd let him escape. Maybe that was a gift he'd give to Leah. But after all that Elliot had done, he enjoyed the notion of him fleeing with his life only to lose it again to something as innocuous as a bottle of wine.

Tate left the drake with the run of the place and slipped back out.

THE END

Acknowledgments

A debt of gratitude to you, the reader, for letting this story in. I hope you don't ever encounter a house guest like Mr Tate.

A huge thank you, as always, to my gorgeous wife, Anne-Marie, who allows me to entertain sociopaths in my imagination from 9 to 5. Also to my supportive Mum and Dad, who gave me the freedom to live in my head from a very early age.

And now to the talented crew at One More Chapter – Hannah Todd, my perspicacious editor, who jumped on this story from first submission; Bethan Morgan, Assistant Editor, who has again expertly guided my project through the fine edit process; Charlotte Ledger, Publishing Director, for co-ordinating and running a tight ship; Melanie Price, Digital Marketing Manager, for her online interviews and quiet magic; Lucy Bennett for such a smart and striking cover; and Claire Fenby, indefatigable Digital Marketing and Publicity Assistant.

And, as ever, I can't underestimate how grateful I am for the time spent by reviewers and bloggers who are such a vital cog in every author's career and convey their passion for books by shouting about the ones they love. Thanks for your generosity online but, moreover, for giving up your valuable time to point readers towards a wealth of great writing. A special salute to Karen Cole, Jen Lucas, Nicki Richards, Claire Knight, Sarah Hardy, Liz Barnsley, Melissa Suslowicz Bartz, Donna Maguire, Zoe-lee O'Farrell, Nigel Adams, Suze-Clarke-Morris, Kaisha Jayneh, Amanda Oughton, The Book Cosy, Louise Mullins, Carole Whiteley, Rachel Broughton, Alison Drew, Magdalena Johansson, Diane Hogg, Martha Cheeves, Joyce Juzwik, Amy Sullivan, Kelly Lacey, Rebecca Pugh, Chelsea Humphrey, Ellie Smith, Steve Robb, Emma Welton, Stephanie Rothwell, Cleo Bannister, Abby Fairbrother, Sheila Howes, Linda Strong, Maxine Groves, Joanne Robertson, Susan Hampson, Malina Skrobosinski, Shell Baker, Fran Hagan, Mandie Griffiths, Jo Ford, Marilina Tzelepi and Scott Griffin. Special thanks also to fellow author and crime writing doyenne, Noelle Holten, for her continued support.

Please swing by my website for all the latest: richardjayparker.com or find me on Instagram (@bemykiller), Twitter (@Bookwalter) and Facebook (@RJParkerUK).